LUNA STONE

THE CURSE OF THE NINE

LALINE'S ASCENSION

The Curse of the Nine
Copyright © 2020. Tethys Night Sky Publishing

Second paperback edition, September 2021

Book cover design and interior layout by *Miblart*
Edited by *Angela Walker*
Blurb by *Fallon Moore*
Typesetting managed by *Fallon Moore*

ISBN 978-0-578802-48-0 (paperback)

Published by Tethys Night Sky Publishing
www.tethysnightsky.com

"Wisdom begins in wonder."

-Socrates

For lovers
of the night sky.

TABLE OF CONTENTS

CHAPTER 1

THE UNEXPECTED SURPRISE

T*his will be an epic adventure!* Selina Kyle Horton thought as she exited the Vancouver airport. Her flight from New York had been seemingly short: a nonstop, six-hour trip of which she hardly slept. How could she? This was her first time traveling alone. Being one with nature and reflection. She could barely contain her excitement.

Her dad, Hollywood actor Brett Horton, video-called her several times. Brett wasn't her biological dad, but he certainly was her father in every capacity her mind could think of. Brett and Kate, her adoptive parents, were white, rich, and incredibly famous to the "genpubs," a word that Selina and her sister Haley liked to think they made up, which meant general public. Selina did not look like her sister. Haley, a thin blond, gray-eyed, tinier replica of their mom Kate did not resemble the deep rich brown, tall, curvy yet toned creature that Selina saw when she looked in the mirror. But how could you measure a family's love based on how they looked? All four of their kids looked different. Miskath, the oldest at 22 and adopted from Sri Lanka, had been the shortest at 5'7". Selina, 20, stood at a stellar 5'10". Haley, 18, stood a few hairs off 5'8", and lastly, the youngest, Brett Jr., 16, towered over them all at 6'1" and growing.

Selina took after Brett the most. During vacations, the two of them bonded over exploring the hiking trails; seeing and hearing things only a person who was *paying attention* could see and hear. Miskath enjoyed nature, too, but the science of it as a working system, which is why he studied ecology at Harvard. Selina and Brett enjoyed the peace of it, the *danger* of it.

The phone buzzed again in her hand. A picture of Brett emerged on the screen. He'd taken his own contact photo. The picture displayed him looking up and to the left; next to his face was his hand mimicking the shape of a phone. She knew that if she didn't answer this time, he'd probably call the airport police. She answered the call.

"Finally! She answers," Brett teased. She looked at her dad. He had dark brown eyes, jet-black hair, and a cleft chin. To Selina, Brett had the look of an NFL quarterback. Despite him being nearly fifty, she could still picture her six-foot-four-inch dad excelling at anything athletic. He kept himself in incredible shape.

She smiled. "Dad, give me time to get off the plane." He returned her smile, making hers even brighter.

"Selina, my darling," he replied, and she knew he was up to something.

"Dad," she laughed, "what did you do?"

"I know you were so excited about traveling alone…" He trailed off.

"Dad?"

"I just thought I'd provide a guide on your adventure."

"Daaaaaaaaaaaaaaaad!" She frowned and stomped her foot in protest. "I'm not going to need security here. I'm not Haley!" she puffed. "I don't have my own YouTube channel. Or social media!!! No one even knows or cares…" She looked away from her phone up to a clear Canadian sky.

"Selina Kyle Horton!" he said in his serious actor dramatic dad voice. "Look at me."

When Haley and Selina were little, their mom Kate doted on them to no end. They'd play dress up, tea party with their mom's most expensive silks and perfumes. With Brett, Selina liked to splash muddy rain puddles. When the rain stopped, they watched the worms inch to the surface of the soil. Selina liked to be a pretty princess for mom, but she loved getting dirty with dad. Haley hated the mud. Haley hated worms. Miskath much preferred reading about worms than seeing them in real time. Their routine was exclusively theirs.

Her heart suddenly filled within her. The thoughts of her childhood and their daddy-daughter adventures swelled her inside like a helium machine would a balloon. Brett could really do no wrong. Selina looked back at her phone to further discuss the alterations Brett made to her trip.

"Selina." Leopold Benton approached her right on schedule, immediately after she ended the call with her dad. Leopold Benton was a thin, shaky middle-aged man with a large, crooked nose and a thinning blonde ponytail. Selina looked at him and always instantly thought of Mr. Burns from *The Simpsons,* although Leopold seemed much younger. It could have been the way he spoke, soft and slow at times with either a fake French or British accent. He switched up throughout the years. For some reason, Brett trusted Leopold.

"I have got quite the adventure planned," he finished. "Do not think of me as a guide. There will be actual guides." She went to disrupt him, but he placed one finger in the air as if to protest. "Your father insisted you wanted privacy, and that is what you will have. Just think of me as the facilitator."

CHAPTER 2

THE MARK OF OBEAH

The drive had been longer than expected. She sat in the back of a rented Jeep Grand Cherokee. Leopold drove quietly. He did not engage in small talk, which is something she generally appreciated from people she didn't know well.

She drifted off into a peaceful doze until she felt the car make an abrupt left. The clock on her iPhone revealed they'd been driving for nearly three hours. She thought about asking him EXACTLY where they were headed, but she decided against it.

The jeep began to reduce speed. In the dead of night (an hour past midnight for sure), she could see a high stone wall. The stone wall opened large enough for a metal gated driveway. On the other side of the driveway, to the far left AND the far right, were two security booths.

Leopold got out of the jeep and walked towards the booth on the left. A uniformed man exited the left booth. Through the gate, Selina watched as the man inserted Leopold's driver's license into a type of portable scanner or card reader. The apparent guard proceeded to take a photo of Leopold then of the vehicle as the other man located in the booth on the far right watched intensely. After what seemed like fifteen minutes of various checkpoints, they both appeared to have been cleared. The man returned into his booth, and both men turned a key simultaneously to open the gate. Selina's original travel plan consisted of renting a room from an elderly woman who ran a bed and breakfast out of her home. This sudden redirection frightened her a bit. She glanced at the man in the left booth, and there was a holstered gun on the man's hip. She immediately brought her eyes back in the car and focused on the view ahead. They drove another 100 yards before coming to a complete stop.

Two women and one man dashed over to offer Leopold assistance. Even in the dark, Selina could see multiple vast properties in the distance. The oldest of the two women scurried to Selina's door and motioned for her to exit. Cold October air blew in. She felt the crunch of a first frost under her boot as she exited the vehicle. *The temperature dropped at least twenty degrees,* she thought to herself as she followed the women into the massive-sized cabin.

Leopold and the man entered shortly after, carrying in their luggage. Only then did Selina realize that none of the staff had been wearing a coat. The women wore quilted silk dressing gowns, with waist scarves. For a brief second, she wondered about their attire. Obviously, they were not guests—but service staff. Why else would they have come to greet her? Yet, the intricate, colorful patterns and embroideries of their garments were more fitting of priestesses. It warranted another glance. The gowns were made up of Mulberry silk, one of the most expensive silk types in the world. Her mind started to recall a detail about tribes and tribal robes, but she dismissed the idea.

"Greetings," an older woman, of around fifty-five or a vibrant sixty, said with a bow and a slight smile. "The master bedroom is one flight up those stairs." She pointed to the ascending stairs behind them.

"My name is Edha." She smiled again, this one more authentic. The woman's grinning light brown eyes transformed her entire face, making her appear ten years younger. "Welcome to *En*

Tutum." Selina removed her glove to return the greeter's hospitality properly.

Instantly after, the smile vanished as quickly as it appeared. Edha's eyes widened at the sight of the visitor's hand.

It beheld a crescent-shaped scar starting from the knuckle of her right index finger curving around to the knuckle of her thumb. Confused by the woman's obvious and awkward staring, Selina looked down and concluded why the woman might have been hesitant to shake her hand.

"It is just a scar," Selina said, visibly offended.

"Apologies, young madam," the older woman uttered after a few long uncomfortable moments of ogling. "I was admiring your stunning bracelet. Is that Peruvian gold?"

"Why yes, it is," she answered excitedly. "You have a very keen eye." Edha nodded in acknowledgment of the guest's observation.

"And are you from Peru?"

"No." Selina chuckled. "Calabasas, California, but I'm actually coming from New York. I go to Barnard College."

Leopold let out a long yawn.

"Selina, let me settle you in your room for the night," he said abruptly. "It is very late, and I'm sure everyone is quite exhausted." Before Edha or the other two could respond, he walked past them holding Selina's things. "Shall we, now!"

he commanded. There was relief on Edha's face. It was true. They all were weary, and it seemed at this point she had no choice but to follow Leopold up the stairs toward her quarters. The room appeared a few meters away as they reached the top of the staircase. Its entry consisted of two twenty-foot massive doors. Both were unlocked and slightly ajar. Leopold impatiently barged in.

The lights were dimmed, yet in low light, Selina could tell that these accommodations were terribly expensive. The master suite included a bedroom, living room, and spa room all in one. She could see an oversized hot tub in an adjacent chamber. A California King four-post bed covered with what she hoped was a faux fur comforter called to her. Just the sight of the bed suddenly made her limbs feel heavy, and body wane. It was all she could do to walk to it. Relief surged through every cell at the very instant her buttocks sat on the cool blanket. She unceremoniously lied back. Hardly, something she'd normally do. She heard Kate's voice in her head. "Even if you're wobbly tired, it is STILL very important to at least wash the day off your face." And Selina wanted to. Sleep had already begun to wrap itself around her. It's cool-silky, black strips of peace spiraled her person until resistance was useless.

Leopold looked at her and shook his head. She still had her boots on, feet still on the ground while her torso rested on a luxurious Viking-style bed. Odd that her coat remained zipped up to the neck, and her cream-colored scarf nicely secured the hood on her head. If he hadn't been a witness to her whereabouts, he would've fathomed she passed out drunk.

None of his business, he supposed. He lingered on for another second, questioning if he should at least remove her boots and coat. Reason clutched him. How could he explain removing a girl's clothing this time of night? The thought frightened him so terribly that he half ran out of her room and quickly closed the door.

CHAPTER 3

SOMEONE WAITS HIDDEN

Purple and white particles descended slowly from a twilight sky, like how cherry blossom trees disperse its pink corollas. *Lavender*, her nose told her mind as the small, very fragrant petals, swayed slightly in the night air in abundance. *Jasmine,* she recalled to herself again as it seemed to rain flowers, carried on a light breeze.

What is this place? she questioned. Immediately, she noticed her dress, thin and beige, silky smooth to the touch at knee level. A style she would never wear willingly. Yet any caution that arose within her quickly swirled away in the aromatic atmosphere. With curiosity as the lead emotion, she kept on.

She stepped hesitantly in a verdant meadow as the pedals blanketed the grass below. Up ahead, she noticed a golden willow tree, its leaves pendulating in the cool air. The closer she got to it, the more she thought of yellow apples; it matched the color of the vines perfectly. Twenty feet ahead of her now. She felt connected to every surrounding molecule. The blades of grass seemed to part before she stepped down on them. The wind picked up and began to swirl the petals all around. White and purple clusters danced around her as if on purpose, landing all over her face and hair, the fragrance intoxicating.

Someone waits hidden for her under the willow's branches. How does she know? It is hard to say. But the sky could have told the flowers. The moon that lies in waiting may have told the wind to carry it on the tip of its breeze. It could even be the tree itself which appeared increasingly and illuminatingly golden, as dusk began. Out in the night air, with a rising harvest moon, there were no secrets.

As she approached, she could no longer feel her feet on the ground. Her consciousness spread far throughout the meadow. A piece of her joined a grasshopper below, leaping from blade to blade. Almost at the same second, she linked with a nearby ladybug flying about searching for the warming sunlight. She shook her head to focus. A connection with the tree ensued. It felt old and feminine to her mind. It wanted her to come closer and see.

"*Meh-Mon,*" something whispered from inside of its branches. The willows parted for her to enter. Inside, on a bed of flowers, lied an animal. Obviously feline, but too big to be a domestic cat. This creature had a strong triangular face. Its coat thickened around its neck the same way it does on a lion. For some reason, it reminded her of someone wearing a white robe. This long-haired cat had a double coat of grays, white (around its neck), and even shades of blue near its underbelly. A lion it noticeably was not. It looked at her affectionately whilst squinting its eyes. Her connection with the creature jolted her. It felt male. It felt human.

She took a few steps nearer. The cat's thick, long, and (also) double-coated tail curled at the tip. It wanted her closer. The tree closed its leafy vines behind her. They were alone. The cat sat upright, similar to the way a gentleman would stand when a lady entered the room. It wrapped its bushy tail around its front paws. The connection to all other things ceased. Only it remained. Above the tree outside: A pregnant orange moon hung low in the sky.

Her eyes saw an animal. A very cute cat with extra fur all over, even its ears, which, like the rest of its body, seemed to be long-haired and double-coated. Her mind raced to identify it; the best she could come up with was a Norwegian Forest Cat, but this feline before her could easily be the size of an adult pit bull. She extended her arm to touch it. It bowed to her and lowered its ears. It welcomed her contact. Her fingers connected to the animal's head and glided down its back; it was pleased by this action. Once more, she reached out and scratched under its chin. The cat began to purr loudly; she felt another jolt of energy that instantly caused her to close her eyes.

With both eyes closed, her mind's eye saw a ghostly man of European origin, British, if she had to guess. He was kneeling before her, shirtless and frail enough to see the bones protrude from his back. He looked up at her; she didn't meet his eyes. She stared straight ahead.

"At last, you've arrived," the stranger said slowly as if barely able to speak. He appeared defeated from a battle long ended. The man lowered his torso and placed his face between her feet; she felt his breath on her heels. His hands cupped the backs of her ankles. The shock of his grip startled her a little. His hands were wet and a level of cold that reminded her of death or dangerously close.

"Who are you?" she asked, a little revolted by the man's ailing appearance. "Stand."

But the man could not stand. He could barely lift from where he knelt. Slowly he resumed his former position, still on his knees.

"Mother," the man whispered up at her slowly. Confused by his choice of words, she looked down upon him meeting his gaze. Her pulse quickened. Her heart began to bang on her rib cage. Dizzy and confused, she could not understand the sudden need to be closer to him. Her knees obeyed her heart despite the confusion. She felt herself kneeling to his level in slow motion. His eyes were a cold crystal gray. They pleaded for forgiveness from a crime she had not yet discovered. The man looked pained, punished, and abandoned to die. As soon as she reached his level, he hugged her. His torso was slick, icy, and rancid against her bosom. His touch, she imagined, could only compare to hugging a cadaver that had been too frozen to rot. The man recoiled as if he heard her thoughts. Visibly embarrassed, he looked at his chest and arms. Quickly, he brought his hands up to cover his face as he began to cry.

"Forgive me, Mother," the man said from behind his hands.

A deep wave of sorrow swirled inside her. It was she now who felt embarrassed. She brought her arms up to hug the man again. He scrambled away, teary-eyed, and ashamed. She felt the urge to crawl to him; comfort him. Although she couldn't recognize his face or his pain, she was beginning to realize that he may mean something to her. How? A feeling. Her heart knew something her memory failed to recollect.

With a wave, the stranger released thin ripples of smoke from his palm. Confused, the girl thought it to be a cigarette in his hand until the mysterious cloud reached her. It affected the earlobes first, and then every inch of her body fizzed until the connection was gone; the man vanished. She'd been returned to the willow tree despite her desire to stay with the gentleman. Selina immediately noticed the cat had been standing upright, covering its eyes with its front two paws.

"Impossible!" her lips mouthed, but even as she spoke, she felt herself separating. As much as she resisted, her consciousness leaped out of the golden willow tree like a movie in speedy reverse. She saw her body lying on the fur-covered, four-post bed of the very expensive room her dad booked her. The first light of dawn sprinkled colors of pinks and violets through the large window. She wanted to look longer and see the sun rise. A pulling began, almost magnetic, interrupting her peaceful view. Then violent turning, circling around her sleeping body the same way water gets sucked down a drain. In a hard-painful crash, her mind reconnected with her body, and she rose up from bed, sweating profusely in the coat, boots, and jeans she fell asleep in.

"What the Frock?" she said out loud to no one. She felt an immediate smile curl her lips, because it was something Kate, her adoptive mother, said in situations of confusion. The thought of her mom calmed her. *Whatever dream that was—it is over,* Selina thought. She could now focus on enjoying the surprise trip her dad arranged.

CHAPTER 4

THE MORNING AFTER

Morning disclosed a much more extravagant accommodation. The entire cabin-style-mansion contained exorbitant furniture. The room adjacent to her bed featured a sixteen-jet hot tub on a mini-stage. As she soaked, she watched the sunrise from the colossal fifteen-foot window. Selina felt like a queen as she swirled around in a percussion of steamy bubbles. Soon, the strange dream she had the night before drifted down the drain along with every trouble. She estimated the measurement from floor to ceiling to be at least twenty feet, and the windows were just as high throughout the property. Light generously spilled in every window but did nothing to warm the chilly breeze nipping at her toes.

She smelled food the minute she opened the tall mango-wood, double doors to her quarters. After a couple steps, Selina arrived at a spiraling, descending flight of stairs. The rose-gold handrail glowed beautifully, unblemished by fingerprints or smudges. Marble white stairs with flicks of gray complimented the golden rail quite nicely, giving it an overall posh appearance. As she walked down the stairs, slowly, her hand could barely grip the banister, as if the architect designed the two-story cabin for a giant.

Aside from the tingles of a cold floor that managed to seep through her thin slippers, she found herself delightfully impressed with En Tutum—particularly by the oversized paintings she passed on her way down to the dining room.

Selina followed laughter into the bright kitchen where Leopold sat at the trestle-styled table, nibbling on a piece of dry toast. The breakfast spread on the counter nearby quickly caught her eye. Fried pieces of Canadian bacon, pancakes, toast, and sausages all were placed decoratively on individual plates and doilies.

"There she is," Leopold muttered with a mouth full. "Come now, breakfast is served quite deliciously." He smiled. Two new women dressed in white polyester uniforms rushed to make a place for Selina next to the jolly fellow. The massive table and chairs swallowed her up, made her feel like a small child sitting in an adult setting. Usually, her experiences were the opposite. In other instances, she felt like the giant, nearly six-feet-tall, standing barefoot.

She'd been hypnotized by the many jams, jellies, and syrups she had to choose from for her toast: strawberry and peach jam, rhubarb orange jelly, grape jelly, maple syrups, and more. The cafeteria at her dorm mostly offered farina and wide varieties of granola. Breakfast for her consisted of a White Chocolate Mocha Frappuccino from Starbucks and maybe a muffin an hour or so later. The breakfast added the final touches to the extravagant morning she'd been already enjoying.

"Eat up," he said excitedly. "You have a big day planned."

"Just me?" she asked, barely able to contain her excitement. "You're leaving?"

"Yes, duty calls, I'm afraid," he stated with a fake disappointment. "I'll return to take you to the airport."

"I'm sure I can manage," she said, trying to persuade him from his role as her shadow.

"Are you sure?"

"Yes."

"But I promised your father," he added. "You know how he is when it comes to you."

"I swear to tell him I drove you away, against your very strong will," she promised. Leopold exhaled with relief. She deemed he didn't want to stay as badly as she wanted him gone.

* * *

Two hours after the wondrous meal she'd eaten, she found herself standing in the exact place she stood the night before, right outside of her luxurious cabin. Daylight told a different tale. Miles and miles of forest spread far beyond the embankment. She could see colors of deep rich greens, yellows, and reds high ahead above the stone walls enclosed around the properties. Behind her, there were similar cabins, four that she could see in various heights and widths.

"It's the same place the Prime Minister takes his daughters," Brett told her proudly when she called him after breakfast. He read about En Tutum in an article about his favorite jazz singer Kitt Wells. It's highly private and highly secure. "You can get to know nature with several renowned outdoorsmen, and then you can lie in the lap of luxury!" Brett continued smiling in a way that twinkled his eyes. And how could she be mad at such a well-thought-out, properly-planned surprise? He knew she shared his love for nature. What better way to prepare her for her own adventures? She smiled back at his smile as she often did. The video call with her dad made her even more excited to start exploring.

Brett loved the idea of group hiking and camping activities with skilled staff. He knew Selina would love it! Both Brett and Kate chose that place, particularly for its discretion among celebrities. Also, its indulgent amenities were lovely.

CHAPTER 5

MR. HORTON'S DAUGHTER

Kent Woodrow, a well-known nature enthusiast and corresponding contributor to National Geographic, earned his acclaim by posting survival videos on the web. He traveled to the deepest, coldest places of the world and recorded himself braving it. Selina and Kent were the same height; a detail Selina noticed immediately once he exited one of the tan Jeep Wranglers that pulled up. He smiled a smile merely meant to be polite.

The explorer before her mirrored every nature man she ever saw on television. Kent wore the Indiana Jones/Jack Hannah fedora, an expensive outdoorsy Gore-Tex jacket covered by a tan nylon utility vest—the kind with multiple pockets. She did not find him attractive. He sported a big square head, rugged face—which resembled a few days without shaving and maybe the seedlings of a salt-and-pepper beard, she thought—but most of all, his dark eyes were oversized and unfriendly.

"You must be the infamous Selina Horton." Kent bowed. "It's such a pleasure to finally meet you. Your father, Mr. Horton, has been a major contributor to my causes." Selina nodded in acknowledgment. As far back as her mind ventured, she remembered her parents as philanthropists. Both Kate and Brett were well-known preservationists. It did not surprise her to learn this.

He'd never seen Mr. Horton's oldest daughter, aside from old photos in even older magazine articles. Her upturned, chestnut-colored eyes shined with amber tints in the setting sunlight. An indifferent expression did little to hide her beauty from him. He drunk in the girl's features, skin that appeared a warm reddish-brown, full peaked, bow-shaped lips, perfectly natural. From the tightly-wrapped curly bun in her hair to her thick, long, and real eyelashes, he realized everything about this girl was natural—unlike some wealthy women he came across, who obtained their beauty through plastic surgery.

Although, he could tell she wasn't the California type. She dressed more like a New Yorker. She wore a black close-fit insulated leather jacket, nice soft yet snug jeans, and dark waterproof Ugg boots.

To be young again, he thought sourly. He concluded her to be at least half his age of forty-three. It's not like he hadn't dated twenty-somethings before, but he knew her father and couldn't risk losing the financial support.

"Some of this journey may be filmed. I must disclose that," he said as if he hated saying it. "I will need your signature of release if you consent to being filmed AND edited in ways that promote the show."

"What show?" she asked, and the look of dread grew more apparent on his face. "I didn't come here to appear on any show. I thought this was a place that respected privacy?"

"It is, Ms. Horton. Selina—may I call you Selina?" She didn't answer. "During any expedition, I like to bring my crew just in case I come across a teachable moment. This wonderful estate afforded me the right to do so, and I could not refuse."

He smiled again, but his eyes did not. The eyes were impatient and agitated. Selina assumed he was used to people being excited to appear on his show. Perhaps he deemed asking for signatures beneath him? She guessed he had to ask her personally out of respect for her father's money. Whatever the case, she knew her answer.

"I won't consent." It never occurred to her to say anything else. The expression of disdain was displayed clearly on Kent's face, with zero attempts to hide it. "I do not want my image anywhere," she continued to state sternly, despite his contempt. A few uncomfortable seconds passed.

She'd gotten pretty used to telling people no. Brett and Kate were famous, well known, and loved all around the world. Selina learned early, although she understood the lure of fame, it was a monster she refused to nurture. She never allowed herself to be photographed, filmed, or interviewed. Mostly all of the media outlets knew to leave her alone; Kent, however, did not get the memo.

"As you wish, Ms. Horton," he said finally. "I can't say I'm surprised. Your dad never wanted to co-host my show either." He stepped closer towards her, entering a proximity only suited for a lover or family. "The camera would've loved you," he whispered, meaning every word. He'd already imagined an episode concept. The eldest Horton daughter, a tall, slim-fit, mahogany beauty in the wilderness for the first time, that alone would've racked up ten million views at least. Her refusal pissed him off a little. He managed to keep a smile on his face, however forced. Maybe if he played nice, she'd reconsider at some point.

Selina hated his proximity to her, more so, the gall of him to invade her personal space. She bunched her toes in her boots to stand firmer and stronger into the ground. She couldn't determine whether his tactics were horrible flirting, or passive-aggressive intimidation. She was not sure. It felt like a challenge, and the Hortons did not back down. So, screw whatever he was saying. The answer would always be no.

CHAPTER 6

THE HARVEST MOON

The October wind banged against her tent. No matter how many blankets she lined her sleeping bag with, she was still very aware that she was sleeping on the cold earth. The branches above her swayed as their leaves rustled and hissed. Outside, the flame to their fire fought hard to remain alive as the wind strengthened.

I do not fear. Fear follows the unknown, and there is nothing unknown out here.

Selina recited a little chant Kate made her and her sister memorize. There'd been an intense thunderstorm on a night their dad happened to be away. Selina, eight at the time, and Hailey, six, cowered under the covers of their parents' humongous bed. When Kate told her little girls it was time to go to their own rooms, both began to cry, afraid of sounds of the thunder and wind.

Each time thunder shook the entire foundation of their home, their mom named the sound.

"The sound you hear is thunder, common in a thunderstorm. Thunder is caused by lightning, air pressure, and temperature. We do not fear what we know," Kate continued. "The howling sound is caused by strong currents vibrating against each other." Kate went on and instructed both girls to identify each scary sound as it occurred, explain why it was scary, and define it. "Fear follows the unknown. I do not fear what I know. Now repeat." Eight-year-old Selina felt a tingle of empowerment right then; suddenly, fear seemed illogical.

Outside in the elements, however, fear seemed very logical! Still, Kate's chant had already set her mind on the road to rationality. She was not alone. There was a total of nine tents outside in the Canadian elements. A reasonable distance away, five Jeep Wranglers stood, filled with extra supplies and extra weapons. The most comforting of all turned out to be the two huge panels of LED lighting installed by the crew for filming at night. Even though the sounds were most unsettling, lights and cameras brought much-needed comfort to her.

* * *

Silence roused her from sleep. Immediately, she noticed the darkness. No fire. No lights. She grabbed the flare gun she stashed under her pillow. As she began exiting her tent, she observed the other tents were gone. The entire campground had changed and the climate also. The wind did not blow as harshly. She looked up and spotted a big red moon lounging lazily low in the sky. Movement in the distance snatched her attention. She recognized the image as it approached.

"You again?" Selina huffed. The cat galloped toward her, happily. Its feelings surrounded the animal like a momentary hue of yellows and oranges.

"You are not safe here," she heard it say in her head.

"How are you speaking to me?" she asked aloud. The whole experience of dreaming and linking to things unnerved her. Strange tingles engulfed her nervous system, neither painful nor pleasant.

"We are connected," it said telepathically and galloped away.

Odd sensations pulsated through the orbital bones surrounding her eyes. She brought both hands up to her face in anticipation of pain.

Tingles. Fizzes. Shivers. There were things happening the girl could not identify—things increasing to the point of climax.

She turned to walk away. Distracted by the myriad of occurrences happening to her at once, Selina tumbled on a twig embedded in the earth.

A hand grabbed her before she hit the ground. She looked up to see the iciest gray eyes staring intensely at her. By instinct only, she attempted to remove her hand from underneath the man's. He latched on. Unexpectedly, the man brought them both upright.

Illuminated by the Harvest moon, she perceived him to be the same man in her dream the night before. His grip no longer slick and cold. More remarkably, he remained poised up and sturdy on his feet. He clutched her hand tightly as their torsos touched.

"You look healed; healthy," Selina said, surprised.

"Your presence here gives me life, Mother," he whispered. She pushed away from him. She did not like being called mother.

"Mother! No way. I am Selina, NOT Mother. Who are you?"

"My name is Augustus," he answered gently.

Augustus stood three inches over her at 6'1". He beheld a much healthier disposition. She found him pleasing to her eyes, handsome even. His black shoulder-length hair, piercing gray eyes, plus the stranger's tall, lean, and muscular body created fluttering in her chest and tummy.

Stranger? He did not *feel* like a stranger.

"Augustus," Selina repeated; her pulse quickened. His energy ignited a strange sensation in her. She failed to identify it.

"We are not safe here," his mind said to hers. "It will begin with the ones you already suspect!" He let go of her hand, and her stomach sank to her feet. The familiar pulling, almost magnetic motion began as it had when they last separated. The connection ceased.

"Another dream," she said to no one, but she didn't believe it. The lights of the original campground blared through her eyelids. She knew she'd returned. Whispers crept by her ears and snatched her attention. It made no sense, but she could hear someone speaking every time the wind hit her tent.

"The girl is harmless. She's from California. I know her parents," a man said.

"You know the people who volunteered to raise her. They are not of her flesh. I saw the mark on her hand. I *know* what it symbolizes," a faint woman's voice argued.

"Lady, you are speaking strangely. Ridiculous, if you ask me!" The man argued.

Selina's eyes shot open. She lay in her sleeping bag, staring at the top. The impulse to unzip herself out of the sleeping bag and run out into the night tingled her arms and legs; she ignored it. Another urge emerging from deep within told her to lie still and to listen *closely*. A shadow leered over her tent.

"The cat's disappearance is not a coincidence," she heard a woman say. "My people feel a presence here. I believe it is your colleague's daughter."

"Quiet down, or you'll wake everyone," Kent Woodrow snapped at a lower tone. His clumsy shadow needed no further inquiry. He stomped when he walked; she knew it was him. Undoubtedly, the woman's identity was also revealed: Edha, the older woman who received her at the cabin. Selina recognized her voice.

"Relax. There was a calming agent in the tea we had you serve." Just as Edha said it, Selina's eyes shot to her thermal, but she remembered filling it with her own blend of tea. She took the other cup to be polite but did not drink it. "A tornado could pass by here," Edha continued. "A spirit would rise before any of these campers; everyone is sleeping deeply."

"You poisoned everyone, even my crew?" Kent accused loudly.

"Poisoned? If we wanted you all dead, you'd all be dead," Edha said flatly. "The forest is such a dangerous place; unpredictable and elusive, Mr. Woodrow."

"Never been more thankful that I prefer scotch," he boasted. "My own special brew!" Kent waited, expecting the woman to laugh or at least humor him with a smile. Edha did neither.

"I expected as much, which is why I've come."

"You came for me, knowing I'd be the only one awake?" he asked. "For what? All this over some missing cat?"

"If you knew how serious a situation this could be, you wouldn't make light of it." She grabbed his arm. "Centuries ago, Satan sent his demons up from hell in the form of animals. These animals or familiars were rewards for his most loyal followers. Mr. Woodrow, a cat is never just a cat, and a girl is never just a girl."

"Holy shit." He yanked his arm back dramatically. Edha smiled. "You're joking, right?" he asked the late-night visitor, but she didn't confirm or deny her claims. "So, what can we do against a demon girl and her cat?"

"If you see the cat, shoot it," she said, sounding further away. "We'll contain the girl at the property. The Hunter's Moon draws near. It must come and go without incident."

Moments inched by, seeming like hours. Eventually, she heard the ignition of one of the Jeep Wranglers rev up. For the first time ever in the years and years of knowing him, she actually *missed* Leopold. She wished she hadn't sent him away. She could've used that extra layer of protection.

The two conspirators left her alone with nothing but the wind banging.

Her dad, the wondrous outdoorsman, bought her the humungous backpack that now lay on the floor of her tent. The Osprey Aether AG 70 had wide cushion straps that slipped over the shoulders. It came equipped with additional straps meant to buckle around the waist for even weight distribution. Sure, it was heavy, but the contents inside could keep her alive for days outdoors.

We'll detain the girl at the property.

Edha's words evoked terror in the girl's spirit. The thought of being detained didn't sit well with her. She hadn't done anything wrong. Something urged her to flee, to escape deeper into a forest she did not know. The thought squeezed her insides. At that moment, she remembered the two guards at the gate and the guns on their hips. The high stone walls surrounding the estates and the taller gated driveway suddenly seemed designed to keep people in as much as intruders out.

These people obviously mistook her for someone else. To what lengths were they willing to go? Kidnap her? Lock her away? Kill her? Canada is not her country. She knew her mom and dad would fight like hell to find out the truth, but who else would care for an unknown college girl's unfortunate demise?

No.

She grabbed her backpack and hoisted it upright. Instincts kept her from drinking their coma-inducing tea. Standing up to Kent had been her gumption alone. Something pulled at her; the thought of braving it alone in the woods until she got to the next town seemed reasonable. She had food, shelter, a weapon, and, most importantly, she had the upper hand.

She grabbed the backpack and clicked the buckle around her waist. Next, she secured both shoulder straps. Finally, she checked her cellphone, and it displayed the word "searching." She turned off her device. If the people after her were bold enough to spike a chamomile brew, they might have installed a service scrambler near the campground. Selina's fervor increased.

I'll just get out of the scramblers range and call my dad, she thought. Once outside of the tent, she patted at her waist to see if she remembered her utility knife. Her fingers grazed the blade in its sheath. Kent's crew supplied the tent and camping equipment for all the travelers. She took the prepacked bag along anyway at her dad's insistence, another detail for corroboration if needed. She found a trail leading away from the lights and the vehicles. The direction undeniably led her deeper into Canadian country. Selina's steps remained as steady as they could on the uneven terrain. Her pathway darkened the further away she trekked from the campground. Soon, there were only peeps of light from a shady white moon above.

"I will not fear," she said to the night and marched on.

CHAPTER 7

AUGUSTUS

The campers woke early, at the first sliver of morning. How lovely they slept. Peaceful, warm, and restful. Kent's three-man crew also exhibited unusually cheery faces.

Kent did not experience the rejuvenating night's rest everyone else raved about. Nightmares plagued what little sleep his mind granted him. Frankly, the bright faces of even his own crew annoyed him. From inside his quarters, he could hear everyone attribute their rest to the great outdoors.

"Kent," Katie, the sound girl, said. "We just did a head count, and that Horton girl is not here." Rumblings of chatter waved over the campground. *When did she leave? Why did she leave?* Relief touched the corners of his headache.

A missing camper meant a total cancelation of the day's events; it was protocol. It was in his written contract as a guide. After he alerted security, he'd return everyone to their respective cabins.

He loved nature. If feasible, he'd be one of the hippy guys that lived in a minimalist hut— no Facebook, no timeline, no video chat. Yet, in order to love nature, he felt responsible for protecting it, which included trying to get other people to love it too! His camping events, survival videos, and social media posts were all intended to get people to help him save nature. Albeit, exhausting as it was, he still couldn't imagine doing anything else.

"While I'm sure Selina is fine," he said in an announcement, "it is protocol that we return to our cabins and let security do their jobs." He suffered through their sighs and protests. "If everyone could please pack up quickly and meet at the Jeeps. We depart in 30 minutes."

He repressed all of the horrific scenarios his mind conjured up. Maybe Edha returned sometime in the night and collected Selina? He thought of calling Brett as a courtesy. Maybe she resisted and they used force? And if he drove to the sheriff, what would he say? An old lady thought a college girl was evil and stole a cat from hell. Selina *could* have wandered off. To curve his own curiosity, he vowed to stop at

Edha's cabin. He needed to go to his own cabin too. Twenty-four hours, he concluded. If the girl is not seen or heard from this time tomorrow, he would call her father. The idea seemed to relieve the tension around his brain. He would have given Edha a 24-hour start.

Surely, he didn't believe in hocus pocus Satan worshiping. Kent believed in his own campaign and what benefited his causes. Edha and her gentleman associate committed to funding an international coalition led by Kent and his team. The deal included start-up monies, fundraisers, and a property to operate business; in return, he would provide worldwide advertisement for all of their estates, including the current one. Waiting a day to call Brett appeared to be the best way to keep everyone's donations coming in.

* * *

Selina walked all night into midmorning. She enjoyed the life of the forest. The trees alone kept her amused; some were massively tall and old, others short and spread out. The colors varied from red to rich browns as the fall foliage cascaded, swirling in the October wind and landing on the forest floor. The leaves on the trees varied from yellow to orange and deep waxy greens. Birds sang their morning praises and hopped from branch to branch happily. Content amongst the cheeps and chirps, she let herself forget about Kent and Edha.

Having no need for it and, at times, forgetting about it entirely, her cellphone remained off. She knew the time of day based on the sun's position in the sky, although mostly shaded by the high red ferns. From what glimpses the trees allowed, Selina estimated the time to be either 11:00 am or noon. Her legs ached a little; to her surprise, the soreness ranked on a level of mere annoyance. She could go much further if she needed to.

A nearby bush rustled. Selina did not notice. Something dashed across her path. She grabbed at the knife clipped on her belt instantly. Movement again, directly ahead.

A red fox approached her cautiously.

The fox bore a bright coat, the color of the setting sun, an exotic mixture of reds, browns, and orange tints. Its underbelly was a soft white, and in her mind, she could envision the sight of freshly fallen snow, the kind that crunches when you step on it. The animal exposed its teeth in an aggressive growl, which, otherwise, may have been alarming if it had not been shaking and shivering. It hunched its head and shoulders down, ready to leap. There was no way to tell the intended direction. Foxes normally did not bother

with people, but this one seemed menacing—
hurt, maybe—or ravenous with hunger.

Boom!

Something exploded out of the bush closest to
her. She swallowed a tornado of air. The sound
struck immobilizing fear in her veins. A large
figure sprang up at such a velocity, it brought
a shower of shrubs and twigs with it while it
soared. The sheer force startled the nearby birds
on their branches. As the leaves propelled to the
sky, the birds let out a warning cry and retreated.
Selina ducked. Such a reaction rustled the trees,
further releasing more leaves. Her first instinct
had been to protect her eyes from the falling
debris. Her body stiffened.

They found me, she thought, fearing this
disruption was a trap set by Edha.

The college student hunched down and ran
off the walking trail. A few feet over, she dove
behind a short fat tree for cover.

"What the Frock!" A smile was already
appearing on her lips. The words worked.
Ten minutes ago, the forest had been filled
with a quiet contentment. The recent events
undoubtedly amused her in a way that left her
nervously excited. Still leaning against the tree,
she realized she hadn't taken a break since she
began walking. Quite the anomaly that she chose
not to explore further until now.

I don't feel like I've been walking for eight or nine hours. She unstrapped the large and *heavy* camping backpack from her waist. The straps slid off her shoulders in an incredible thud.

Shouldn't my shoulders ache a little? Selina's mind began to race.

When had she eaten last? Taken a sip of water? Sat down for a rest? The big bag that contained all of her sustenance—shelter, water, food—remained untouched. She hadn't even been wearing gloves this whole time!! Calmly, the girl placed a hand on one of her cheeks. Both hand and cheek were room temperature warm. It couldn't be explained. Indifferent to the cold? Indifferent to being alive? Selina failed to recall the last time she relieved herself. Panic clutched her rib cage, squeezing the air out of her body. There'd been no distinction of reality.

"Is this a dream?" Selina wondered

"It's not a dream," a voice spoke in her mind. A voice she recognized.

"Why can't I see you?" she said aloud. "Show yourself!"

The *Norwegian Forest*-looking cat strolled toward her, walking around the tree she hid behind and sat at her feet. How larger the cat appeared related to the fox she'd just seen. Upon meeting its gaze, *she knew* what had leaped out of the bushes at such strength. The cat's presence calmed her panic entirely.

"This is a dream then?" Selina said aloud. "You've only ever appeared in my dreams."

"Long ago, my people lived in the forest. To travel long distances. As a gift, we received an enhancement for protection against the elements," the cat conveyed to her mind.

Selina slinked down the tree until her bottom touched the earth.

"How are you able to talk to me? Is it me? Do I have a brain tumor?"

"Selina," it sighed, "we are connected, linked mentally."

"Are you the cat from hell? A familiar? Is that why they are after me? Because of you?"

"You ask many questions," it stated to her mind. "May you permit me to answer them all?"

Selina did not answer. She figured if the cat could speak into her mind, it could tell what her silence meant. Now was as good a time as any to set up camp and take a rest. She supposed its answer might take a while.

"Long ago, my people lived in the forest. We possess a gift bestowed unto us by faeries, servants of the spirit world. The enchantment prevents us from succumbing to the elements. Every child born from the blood of our people inherits it. Through you, I am able to wield it; share it. I haven't felt it in this form in centuries."

"The form of a cat, you mean. Do you serve Satan?" the girl asked as a matter of fact.

Selina began unpacking her tent. Completely entertained as if hearing a story with her headphones on (*that is what a voice in her mind felt like*), she continued to listen while setting up shelter.

"No. I am no familiar," it said sternly. "I am not a demon. I am a cursed man; a prisoner, sentenced to walk the earth in this form: as a cat." It stopped confused as it watched Selina lay the tarp foundation for her North Face series 3, two-person tent. Of course, it never heard of North Face or witnessed a tent of this kind erected so quickly. The worry of having sufficient shelter was a worry no more. And any relief to the task at hand was a bonus to them both.

"The enchantment has returned. Through you, Mother, much is possible."

"Don't call me that!" Selina griped. "You sound ridiculous. As ridiculous as me talking to a cat with my thoughts." She pulled out her sleeping bag and tossed it inside the newly erected sanctuary; the backpack got tossed in next. Weariness seeped into her limbs, and every movement took more of an effort.

She entered their shelter buttocks first and removed her shoes.

"Are you coming in?" the girl said impatiently and regretted it immediately. She would rather have the cat inside with her, instead of outside subjected to predators. The cat hopped in the entrance as if it understood her reservations. She zipped them both in.

She ate two beef jerky packages and their accompanied sticks of cheese. She offered the cat her third stick; it declined. She ate out of habit. Hunger did not return to her; however, fatigue intensified.

Moments later, the girl wrapped herself as tightly as she could in her sleeping bag. Her new companion rested at her feet. She could feel the animal's body on her toes. The day's trek left her body in need of rest. Every blink lasted longer. Sleep was inevitable.

"Why am I so sleepy now?" She yawned. "A moment ago, I was fully alert."

"The long trek left your body in need of recovery. You can rest, Meh-Mon. This shelter is cloaked. It is safe from those that seek us to harm. No one shall enter while you slumber. Rest, Mother …"

* * *

Sunset burned the last of daylight out of the sky. Its lingering rays brightened up the tent and shined an array of shadows on Selina's closed eyes.

"You are a lovely sight, if I may be so bold." That voice aroused the girl out of her lingering slumber. She awoke to discover Augustus lying beside her, his head propped up by his arm. Her companion's large, penetrating gray eyes stared deeply into hers as if admiring a treasure. A flush of heat sizzled the base of her neck, beginning by the earlobes. These encounters always made her feel like static took over the blood in her veins. Sizzles and fizzles bubbled underneath her skin. In the midst of all this occurring, she'd still been very aware of his proximity to her. Nervousness stopped her smile at the eyes.

"Augustus." She quivered, unsure of what to say. Everything, even speaking, drained her. "Is this your true form?" He reached for her hand and squeezed it. The man's touch set her neurons ablaze as if he alone knew the inner workings of every cell and helix within.

"The Hunter's Moon draws near. I'm sure you feel your magic awakening. Do not be afraid. I hope to explain everything by then."

Is this my magic? she wondered to herself. *Everything is so immediately intensified. I cannot focus on a single thread of thoughts around him.* Fluttering in and about the chest flustered her further. Augustus's touch set her skin on fire.

"It's close, and when it comes, all uncertainties will fade into the frost," he whispered, barely using his voice at all.

Selina couldn't reply.

"You are my liberation and I yours." He gently squeezed her hand again.

"I don't understand any of this," Selina said. "But I want you to stay." Their fingers interlocked.

"Rest now, Meh-Mon. I plan to stay, Selina. I will give my life to stay." He let go of her hand and caressed her face. Darkness took her in its clutches to rest some more.

Selina slept all day and into the night. She felt a tickle on the tip of her nose. The cat rubbed its whiskers across her face to gently interrupt her snooze. It wanted her to unzip the tent and let it out. Once fully awake, the two of them exited their hideout to survey the area.

The moon above provided very little light. Once done with nature's call, she decided to look for a flashlight in her massive bag. Exploring the backpack further, she located a battery-operated kettle, small, canned-goods, and granola bars. Brett thought of everything with care. She offered Augustus a small can of dry, flaky tuna. Both inhabitants nibbled at their food in the dark. The girl decided not to travel further until dawn. She reentered the sleeping bag.

"What happened to you?" she asked the cat. "Assuming everything that's happening is real, and you *are* Augustus. Why were you cursed?"

"It is a long story," it answered.

"We have some time."

CHAPTER 8

FEARED DEAD

Kent swashed around a shot of alcohol in the glass he'd just been offered, visibly hesitant to drink it.

"The scotch is fine," Edha grumbled. "I need you relaxed, Mr. Woodrow." He ignored the older woman sitting across from him at the $20,000 ebony Macassar table in her dining room. The entire mansion-styled cabin shared the dining room's decadence in pricey antique furniture. The matter perplexed him. He didn't understand her wealth. Yes, her associates owned many properties all over the world, but how? Edha did not come across to him as a real estate mogul. She spoke and dressed like a high-ranking tribeswoman, a priestess or queen of an ancient people. He met a few along his travels.

"Are you listening?" the woman snapped. Mostly, as a reaction, he brought the cup up to his mouth and swallowed all its contents.

"Happy." He winced. "All gone." Kent half-smiled. The incredibly aged whiskey unveiled a rich potency that made it intense even for him, a regular drinker.

"The girl is still missing," Edha continued. "It's troubling."

"Maybe it's time to call law enforcement," Kent replied, helping himself to another shot.

"Don't be a fool," she bashed. "We promise our clients a safe nature adventure. The publicity alone would hurt us some, but it is certain to end *you*." Kent looked up, confused. "Yes, technically, all of our guests were released to you; they signed waivers. Legally, our estates will be fine."

"You're not gonna pin this on me," he protested. "My team found footage of her leaving the campsite alone. Its blurry feed, but it's noticeably clear it's her and *by herself*."

"Who else is responsible?" Edha asked.

"Why would anyone just get up and walk into the night without so much as a flashlight?"

"That question is meant for you, Mr. Woodrow. The girl may have had help. We know about your dealings with her father," the woman insinuated. "I divulged my suspicions about the girl, and in a few hours, she just disappeared."

"I haven't called him. I'm dreading that call. How do I tell him his daughter had been missing for nearly a day, and no one did anything? No police, no search team. Brett will have the Mounties up here in no time." He poured a third shot. "Dear God, just what did I sign up for?"

"The Blood Moon is tomorrow night," Edha stated.

"What significance is that to the situation?"

"No one, not even law enforcement, will go into those woods under a moon like that," Edha said as a matter of fact.

"A person's life is at stake! Who cares about a moon?"

"The locals. The Townies. I do. And my staff."

"You've gotta be shittin' me!" he yelled. "This is a hundred-million-dollar compound, and all of you fear a fucking *red* moon?"

"What you call fear, we see as respect. We honor the traditions of this place and its customs," the woman lectured, annoyed. "You should know more about that than I." She looked away. He'd lost her respect. "You must go. If the girl is in peril, you must be the one to save her." The scotch calmed Kent's inner rage from exploding to the surface. He tried his best to express himself calmly.

"It's just a little above freezing, without a fire, food, and water; even I would have trouble surviving out there alone," he managed to say very calmly. "This is less about a rescue and more about recovering remains at this point. And to wait another day? Even a couple of more hours is inhumane," he cautioned. "Enough about moons and devils. What scares me more is having a person shivering themselves to death in the night."

"It is decided. Do what you must to find the girl."

"Me? It's easily fifty miles of forest between this place and the other counties. It will take me two days to find her alone. You will not ask for volunteers?"

"As you can see, it's too much of a risk. No one will jeopardize being out there at that time. You are the expert. None of our guests will be harmed."

"What about the two guards with guns? Don't you think I should have security?"

"Those men are needed at their posts. You may have their guns, but not them. Please understand, no one will go with you. It will be you or no one."

Kent snatched the bottle of scotch. He brought it up to his lips and let the golden liquid pour into him as he greedily gulped. If he concentrated, he could see the headlines:

American College Girl, 20, Missing in the Woods; Feared Dead.

All his efforts to promote nature as a wondrous and worthy oasis would be undone. And it would be no man's wonder why she just walked into the night. The nerve of this girl to die and ruin his livelihood by this stupid sniveling action. So stupid, it appeared *purposeful.*

Realization rushed upon him like a putrid avalanche. The only way to save his cause would be to find the girl; rescue her, keep her from freezing to death or worse. In one defeated motion, he slammed the bottle of scotch back on Edha's table and headed towards the door.

In an absolutely desperate utterance, he said, "I want those guns delivered to me in ten minutes. I leave in twenty."

Even with his back to Edha, Kent could see the old woman smiling brightly, displaying a disgusting amount of satisfaction and amusement. The death of Selina will drive his legacy to rubble and ruin. How could he ask people to protect a place when he couldn't protect her? So stupid, it had to be deliberate! If luck was on his side, he planned to find the girl before the moon rose tomorrow. He let himself out, slamming the door behind him. There was much to do and little time to execute the necessary tasks.

CHAPTER 9

LET US HOPE IT DOES NOT COME TO THAT

"Did you hear?" Edha asked her associate, obviously eavesdropping in the next room. Charles Elkins skulked toward the room slowly and without sound. Mr. Elkins possessed the distinguishing looks of a highly intelligent, well-accomplished elder; tall, well-spoken, charming even, and always formally dressed in a suit. Despite the man's elder status, his full head of thick silver hair and well-groomed beard often grabbed the attention of many of the female guests.

"Do you trust him to do as instructed"? Charles asked, his voice deep and commanding.

Edha, still flaunting a smile, turned her face to hide it. It pleased her to frustrate Mr. Woodrow.

"By toying with his emotions, you are toying with his outcome and ours," he chastised.

"He looks to lose his life's mission…"

"And we stand to lose our lives if Augustus is freed. The Aprīcōrum is not likely to forget our oaths." Edha's blood ran cold at the mention of the ancient ones.

"Charles, do you think that girl has the power to free him? You know the strength it took to imprison the nine. A force like that does not exist in this world. Not anymore."

"You speak the truth," Charles admitted. "Yet I feel something churning up the worry in me. The cat's disappearance is unsettling. I sense an inexorable danger approaching."

"The cat escaped our grounds many times. He has no power in that form." Charles grumbled something Edha could not understand.

"Give your woodsman the stun gun," he said eventually. "The magic of Augustus's curse keeps this place running; we need the cat alive. Plus, we don't want to risk killing anyone else out there."

"As long as we collect the remains, the curse will continue," Edha added. "The spirit remains with the corpse until its bones are dust. Quite a long while."

"Kill the cat as a last resort, then," Charles instructed. "Just pray to your gods that the girl is not Meh-Mon." Edha waved his words away. "If you are wrong, there will be no inch of this earth we could hide from them."

"I know," Edha said solemnly. "Let us hope it does not come to that."

Charles walked out of the room as quickly and as silently as he entered, leaving Edha alone with her thoughts and concerns.

Edha caught a glimpse of her own reflection on a polished silver vase placed on the table as a centerpiece. *Still attractive,* she thought. Her light brown eyes (that appeared gray in perfect moonlight) still shone with their exotic vibrancy. The red tints in her thick auburn hair were even more apparent near the flickering candle. She reminisced to a time when her little feet ran through the Bazaar in Khujand, Tajikistan.

If she closed her eyes, she could see the women lined all around wearing colorful headscarves with marvelous patterns. Her mother, Anahitha, worked as an apprentice to a baker.

Caşmoni nur (чашмони нур) Eyes *of Light* is what the patrons called her. Buyers hovered over the fresh naan bread, katlama, and sambusa, which were pastries sometimes filled with meat.

Little Edha watched the wives and daughters come and go, garbed in bright embroidered dresses.

Anahitha cleaned up the shop every night, and before dawn, she rose every morning to help bake the many goods they'd hope to sell. Sometimes, when the shop did well, the owner and his wife tossed some coins their way. Outside of those times, Anahitha labored to occupy a small dirt room located at the far end of the shop. Despite not having money and being narrowly homeless, she never felt more loved.

Only in her deepest of worries did she revisit this period; before her father ripped her out of her mother's arms at age thirteen. Before the Aprīcōrum. Before the nine inflicted chaos on the world and changed life as she knew it.

In distinct silence, she allowed herself full access: the smells, the sounds, and even the happiness to deluge her reality fully.

CHAPTER 10

AERALEE AND THE CURSED NINE

"It is a long story."
"We have some time."

"I must tell three tales. All three are vital to understanding my origin, my power, and my punishment. In the end, you will unconsciously make a choice to either condemn me to loneliness or remain with me; it must be your decision knowing all the information. I only ask that you do not interrupt. I must get through it all quickly." Selina nodded and closed her eyes to focus on Augustus's voice, the only thing left of the man punished to walk as a cat.

"Many millennia ago, before any measurement of time existed, the inhabitants of Earth differed greatly from today. The forest remained a magical place for fear and fantasy. There were beings living in the woods that fed on the flesh of humans. Also, creatures so beautiful, one gaze upon them captured your heart forever.

"This story is of Aeralee, the first Meh-Mon of my people. Aeralee, queen mother, fashioned many names and titles throughout the generations. We heard many tales of her beauty, bravery, and strength. Every hero, I suppose, was once a broken soul. Perhaps I shall begin there.

"Aeralee, born of modest people, entered a modest marriage. She, herself beautiful enough, appeared regular, with common brown eyes and long yet ordinary black hair. As you guessed, the lighter-haired maidens were saved for royalty back then.

"She loved her husband as best her heart could as part of her family's arrangement. She cooked. She tended. She cleaned quite well, but time revealed a rather important duty she failed to fulfill. Twelve moons passed, and no baby arrived. With both sides of their family shamed and enraged, the future almost guaranteed servitude for the motherless wife. In those days, a woman who could not breed did not have any worth. It meant certain death, but her husband had not the heart to end his wife's life. Instead, he dragged her miles into the deepest, densest part of the forest and left her. Aeralee, 19, rejected by everyone she knew, settled into a place she was taught to fear. And what happened next, no one did expect.

"The land adopted her. From the budding flowers on the ground, to the towering trees in the sky and every bird, ant, and deer in between fell in love with Aeralee. Each morning she joined her winged friends in a song. The orphan's love brought a joy to their home. She spoke to the animals, cared for the wounded; something as small as a browning leaf received attention and nutrients from the foreign girl not native to the forest. In return, the community protected her, sheltered her, hid her from travelers, returning her love as best it could. This went on for a while a few months before the season turned.

"Once winter arrived, a terrible storm blanketed the country. Many died. The blistering cold outwitted Aeralee, who had no protection and no way to shield herself. As she lay, mere hours away from her final frozen slumber, a faery came, summoned by the desperate pleas of the animals. Faeries appeared in many forms. Sometimes, they were small, winged creatures, the size of your hand from wrist to the tallest finger; other times, they appeared as human children unwinged and very beautiful. All were spirits, sent by the gods of the forest. This faery took the shape of a little girl, five or six years of age.

"One by one, the trees, the animals—even the snow itself—spoke of Aeralee's worthiness to live and begged the spirit to spare her life. The faery, overcome with urgency, rushed to the dying girl's side. It studied Aeralee as she lay, riddled with frostbite bruises and other skin discolorations. It declared that the raven-haired young woman, the one dying before them barely clothed and barefoot, earned a reward from the gods. That day, the faery bestowed a gift: an enchantment aimed to protect her from the elements. As long as Aeralee shall live, she will never again succumb to the winter's icy clutches. She will no longer perish from heat, cold, wind, or water. The magic of the forest and all of its spirits will protect her.

"The testimony of the woodland creatures captured the curiosity of the small being. The lingering faery found itself increasingly twitterpated by Aeralee's kindness. It remained long after its completed task, hidden and undetected by the recovering woman. It waited to witness her morning song, and after hearing it for the first time, it ached in anticipation to hear it again the next morning.

"Winter dredged on with a callous brutality. Unaffected by the cold, Aeralee went about her days aiding the hungry, finding patches of green under the ice and snow to feed the deer and rabbits. It watched in awe of her happiness despite the everyday struggle to find food and then share with the others.

"Spring arrived shortly thereafter. The faery failed to return to the spirit world. Instead, concealed from sight, it joined her song silently each morning. It helped her find food each afternoon, and at night as she slept, it studied her face and expressions. It had not understood love before her. The selflessness displayed by the girl never occurred anywhere. Its longing surpassed far beyond curiosity. It knew a drastic action neared.

"The faery amassed all its magic and favors from the gods. It begged to appear to Aeralee in the form of a young man. Usually, a faery appeared as a child to humans for safety. But this faery did not want a mother's love from Aeralee. He showed himself to her: a tall, beautiful, thin young man, similar to her age. The faery sang her morning song with a zealous passion, entering all the emotion and the pent-up desire that matured within it, since it first laid eyes on her. Aeralee was powerless to resist the splendor it held for her.

"Their sixty-year union produced over twenty children. In addition to an enchantment, the faery also gifted Aeralee her biggest wish of all: the gift of Meh-Mon; Mother. Together, a new race emerged. Your folklore would identify them as elves, but that is incorrect. There is no name in your language to identify me correctly.

"Their children became mates of other faeries in the spirit world wishing to become mortal for a lifetime.

"I am a descendant of Aeralee. My people came from magic and developed it acutely, and although we evolved somewhat from how she lived, we stayed in the forest. We lived there, believing it was a great honor to do so. And it is."

~ S t o r y   # 2 ~

"In your time—in today's time—wealth is defined as the accumulation of money. The children go to school, learn trades to ultimately earn great sums of it. Their parents work for a wage, and this wage buys them the things that show wealth. In my tribe, to be wealthy meant to have power. And by power, I do not mean thrones, with armies and war. I mean *abilities*.

"This is what we knew as wealth: the ability to adapt and survive circumstances in which others cannot. We did not have currency. The forest did not *belong* to us. Our possessions were based on the powers we accrued. Our fortunes came from the size and longevity of our dynasties. It is a foreign concept to explain even for me. I hope it is clear enough for the purposes of this story.

"When I was not yet an adult, a gift was given to me by the spirits of the land. I could reach my hands into dry, barren earth and create life. At first, it began with little seedlings and mossy patches. Soon and with many counsels, I could grow small amounts of vegetation. If ever the cruelty of a winter stripped us of food, my wealth remedied the problem for weeks. Your eyes ask *how*. The elders worshiped the forest. We were descendants of spirits; their magic lived on in us far after they drifted too far to visit."

Selina wanted badly to ask questions, but she did not interrupt.

"The wind does whisper to those with adept ears. The rain sings, and the blizzards howl; its energy alive. It compels me still, but I am trapped in this form and cannot answer." He stopped for a few seconds, overcome with a sadness visible in his eyes.

"My sister fell in love with a dying man. The man, Jackson, stood 6'6", with blonde hair at the shoulders and a brawn of three men combined: certainly, three of me. He'd been a decorated soldier to an American army. In a war, one he wouldn't or couldn't name, he suffered a mortal injury. Fearing the desecration to his remains, he ran far away from battle into the woods. He ran until he fell, then he crawled until he no longer had any sensation in his arms and knees. And there, on a mossy tree stump; in the woods so dark and closed he couldn't see the sky, Jackson decided to die. Except he wasn't alone.

"His body lay still while his life force dwindled. His blood soaked the leaves of the earth where my sister hid. She'd been running away from the battle.

"At first sight, the sadness and peace in the man's eyes pulled at her very core. Jackson looked back at her unafraid even though he must've been in terrible pain. My sister fell in love with him at that precise moment. His consciousness faded maybe for forever, and my sister shattered at the thought of never knowing him.

"She begged the forest to spare him. She offered herself, her soul, and the gifts given to her by the spirits as an exchange for his life. It took nothing; nevertheless, Jackson survived.

"My sister Abigail nursed him back to health. Overcome with her selflessness, he abandoned his oath as a soldier and made a new oath to her. He, a man of nobility and loyalty, never aimed for personal aggrandizement. Winning wars didn't seem as important as winning her affections. Jackson pledged his life and his heart to her. Happily, he renounced all his worldly possessions and his entire way of life to join her in the forest. Her heart latched on to his and refused to let it stop beating. Retelling their story now, it sounds like a fairytale come true. Yet, his arrival led us both down a path of damnation. It pains me to admit it, but my sister—all of us, even Jackson—may be better off if he just died that day. But I digress."

~ Story #3 ~

"In time, Jackson noticed that he too possessed a gift. Rapidly, as their commitment grew, the man discovered he projected a healing energy. The elders called it the *touch*. Abigail, one of the women we referred to as *Mother,* somehow propelled her gifts unto her new husband—an outsider who knew nothing of the spirits we worshipped.

"Jackson and I developed a kinship. I accepted him as my brother and came to love him as such. It *all started* with him. Together we noticed a surge in our strengths when combined. Alone, my gift fed my people for weeks, with Jackson, for months. His gift grew too. Later around the others, I learned to grow whole trees, rock formations, possibly even mountains.

"One night, I felt a strange energy in the air. Befuddled, I scoured the night to find its source. Jackson and I found the foreign traveler easily, as if drawn to him somehow. Luciano, a Portuguese master of alchemy.

"The three of us felt an immediate influx of power. Our gifts intensified in the presence of others with gifts. Together, we were fixed in a state of elation. We decided to leave our home and travel with Luciano. Our trio avowed to embark on a beneficent journey: feed the hungry, heal the sick, and so on. It seemed selfish to keep our ability native. Despite the good Jackson and I planned, my family disagreed, especially Abigail. Yet even her caution disintegrated against our ambition.

"Luciano proposed we seek out other souls gifted with similar abilities. Very quickly, we were a party of seven, and then the word spread to every shadow and watery crevice that we were the wealthiest beings on the planet.

"We were seeking power beyond any of our imaginations. Godlike power. Jackson and I intended to save the world—him healing the sick and me feeding the hungry in our travels. The more men joined us, the more we deviated from that task. We all were drunk with a force we were not ready to obtain. When our outfit reached seven, the fighting among us begun; driven by greed and intoxicated with abilities never seen on this earth.

"We were not all good men, Selina. Some of us sought power for destruction. Masayori, a Japanese monk turned murderer, master of battle and meditation, committed depraved acts in our name. He sought vengeance. He killed thousands, obliterated whole regions—the men, the animals, and trees alike. And we helped just by being close to him. He fed off our powers to wipe out an entire empiric palace. The elders had had enough. Abigail begged for us to return home. She knew all of us were headed to a fate worse than death. A punishment so severe as to last hundreds of years.

"The Aprīcōrum, an ancient group of powerful elders, said to be direct descendants to the god of light, captured us. A public trial ensued. A verdict was handed out. Each of us was sentenced to walk the earth as some of its *other* inhabitants. They transformed us into beasts and separated us all over the world. The punishment intended to teach us to respect the earth. Ironically, my part in the massacre summed up to be mild curiosity. I possessed no mal intent, which is why I am walking the earth as a cat and why I was sentenced to this place as a prison. In comparison to the others, it appeared to be a kindness but still a punishment, nonetheless. In this form, we have no power. Death of the beast will not restore us back. If this body dies, I will be lost forever.

"I fear them dead. I fear all of them dead; the elders, the men who trapped us in these bodies are long dead, and only I remain. Until you."

Selina stayed silent for a few moments.

"You called your sister *Mother.* Why?" she asked.

"Mother is the embodiment of life. Mother Nature. Mother Earth. Each member of our party had their own version of Meh-Mon. My sister's love gave birth to a new Jackson, one with gifts and strengths. Aeralee, the first Meh-Mon, her love bridged a gap between the human world, spirit world, and animal world.

"You are also Meh-Mon, if not yet then soon."

∗ ∗ ∗

Kent thought it best to begin at the campground. His video feed recorded the direction Selina headed before she walked out of range. Unfortunately, he knew the vehicle he borrowed just became unsuitable for tracking the girl. He then pursued his target on foot. *How far could she really have gone,* he thought to himself, *on only a day's start?*

His experience afforded him the capability to maneuver twice as fast in this terrain. After all, he survived the woodlands, jungles, and forests that were less explored; the ones that didn't have walking trails and weren't thought of as possible tourist attractions. Kent's confidence increased.

Of course, I'll find her without much difficulty, he reassured himself. He smiled and quickened his pace without noticing. All of the worries plaguing him at Edha's cabin crumbled away. He held his high-powered flashlight and shined

5,000 lumens (a measure of the total quantity of visible light) into the country. Dead or alive, he swore to find her.

CHAPTER II

THE BRIDGE

Morning arrived gently, gradually brightening the sky from an indigo dawn to fleshy pinks and blues. Selina witnessed it in silence. Its beauty rendered her incapable of any other functions.

"Even as this perfect morning begins, the forest speaks of tonight. The Blood Moon. A time when the earth, sun, and moon totally align so perfectly, a magic happens," the cat said to her mind. He gazed up at the mahogany beauty sitting beside him. Daylight illuminated Selina's face and hair, flooding her with a goddess-like poise. Her gaze fixed. His heart smiled, although the face he wore could not. Many of his human senses did not function. The true punishment had been allowing him to keep his mental faculties despite changing bodies.

The cat lacked the vocal cords in which to speak human language. He lacked the fingers to operate tools. The cat's body proved to be an inferior substitute to his previous one in the ways he needed. He still suffered from the memories of people he knew long dead. Many centuries passed, and yet his sister's screams still plagued him. The moment they were sentenced and the look in Jackson's eyes were as clear as if it occurred yesterday. As a cat, he still suffered the consciousness of himself. His consciousness was suspended in perpetual regret and torment. Suffering remained his only constant. Yet looking up at Selina as she watched the day begin with such respect and contentment gave him a peace, he'd forgotten existed.

Her mere presence inoculated him with a hope he dared not name. He never learned love in his natural life. He imagined only love could silence the agony he carried. He mumbled a secret prayer to his gods; he prayed she chose to remain with him.

The evening Selina arrived; he felt her energy immediately. Mere moments prior, he walked along the stone walls, his heart, and thoughts heavy with despair. It came to him easily. The wind carried the news of her arrival through the leaves, into the cracks of the stone walls, and finally to him. It felt soft across his face like a lover's caress. *"Mother,"* it whispered to Augustus's eager ears. For joy, his heart leaped.

He did not know how long he prayed for the forest to forgive him. Years blurred into decades then centuries. A seedling of hope nestled in the far corner of his mind. The forest had not spoken to him since his punishment began. The link between him and the land severed. Selina barely passed the security checkpoint, and already his ability to connect to nature was restored. He knew someone had come. His certainty began with a slight increase in his own abilities. Perhaps, he possessed a minuscule amount of power, and Selina's magic increased his own.

Our gifts intensified in the presence of others with gifts.

With what little flecks of magic Selina's presence awarded him, he decided to perform the *"brycg,"* what is known now as a bridge. It establishes a mental link between two magical beings. The first attempt failed. He hid behind the stairwell as she followed the escort to her quarters. He sent out the first link to her mind. Her proximity made it easy to focus his thoughts on connecting to her; however, it only succeeded in making her fall asleep.

Augustus tried again while she slept, remembering an elder told him the mind is more susceptible in dream states. The link began once she touched him. During the brycg, he learned two things:

First, Selina did not know of the strength within her. Just the act of linking with her restored small amounts of his magic. Not nearly enough to free him. The cat's body could not house the force needed to release him. Second, he knew she'd be in terrible danger. If he could feel her power, he knew Edha would. Just as he knew they'd kill her whether she knew how to use her powers or not. Augustus decided right then to protect her. Even if it meant his life.

CHAPTER 12

THE ASCENSION

After an exceptionally light breakfast, Selina packed up. For a moment, she allowed herself to pretend it was a regular camping trip. Other than the cat who could speak into her mind, and a servant woman out to kill her, this would be the best camping trip she'd ever gone on. She felt safe in the forest. She felt safe with Augustus.

"Tonight, I will propel you to the celestial plane," the cat stated seriously. The girl returned a look of utter confusion.

"Tonight, before moonrise, we must conduct a sort of launch. I will push you into the nebula realm," it restated.

"Like in space?" the young woman asked, puzzled.

"Not quite. Remember, tonight's blood moon will be in perigee-syzygy, forming the perfect alignment and opening a doorway between worlds."

"Why would I need to reach there?"

"To be born anew," the cat answered sternly. "We will need some herbs, stones, and a safe place to ascend."

"Wait. Do I get a say?" she interjected.

"No. It is being asked of me to do this. It must be done. I do not question the forest when it speaks to me. I ask you to assert the same trust."

"Trust in the F-O-R-E-S-T," she said, emphasizing on forest. "Trust the forest when it speaks?" she asked again.

"They anointed me a great honor. I've been chosen as your guide. If you have a problem with trusting the forest, can you trust me then?"

"Hmm, the forest or a cat?"

"A man," the cat stated loudly, its voiced boomed in her mind. "A man cursed as a cat. Trapped, really." It sighed as if reminded all over again of its punishment.

"I do trust you," she said quickly. "None of this makes any sense. Normally, I am not the kind of person to explore the impossible. But something is driving my spirit also—a kind of summoning. I cannot explain it. But it feels urgent."

"It is," the cat agreed. "Let us begin gathering all that will be needed."

* * *

The so-called ascension felt more like descending. Like free falling. She imagined it like jumping out of a helicopter, dropping thirty feet, and landing gently into a different dimension, another realm of reality. The air around her carried a sweeter scent, something familiar, but she could not recall. She rose from the ground and noticed the trees around her differed. Upon an initial glance, the trees were shorter than those in the Canadian forest, some a little taller than eye level. The tree closest to her bore yellow and orange oval-shaped, hanging fruit, its branches thin and low enough for her to reach out and investigate the tree's production. The orange fruit bared a shape similar to a sweet potato, yet its exterior felt hard like an outer shell. The leaves of the tree were low, wide, and well-moisturized. *It's a tropical tree,* she thought to herself.

"I loved to pick fruit from the cocoa tree," a woman said frankly, in a Caribbean-French accent. *"Perhaps this is why we are here."*

Selina looked behind her and noticed a tall, brown-skinned woman wearing a loose-fitting beige dress. Startled by another presence, she crouched down, hoping to conceal herself.

Selina watched the woman study the fruit from the tree. Selina realized the woman resembled herself in height, fitness, and facial similarities.

"Do not hide, my child," the woman said loudly. "Time does not allow for fear." She raised her arm and motioned for Selina to get closer. "Come now, let me show you why we have come to this place."

The older woman smiled, and Selina noticed the woman's eyes resembled her own. More than that, it had been how the smile made her feel inside. The same feeling of sipping hot chocolate while the marshmallows tickled her nose: wholesome, warm, and familiar. In a strange state of consciousness, surrounded by cocoa trees and evergreens, she felt at home.

"I am Elodie." The woman turned to reveal long, coarse, Z-shaped curls spiraling down to the small of her back. "You were born on the island of Martinique, by the black sandy beaches and mountains."

"My mother, Kate. She told me—"

"You did not know your mother, child. Please. Let me finish." Selina nodded for Elodie to continue.

"Months before you were born, travelers flooded the city. Men from the north. Researchers determined to prove the existence of Obeah. It is what they knew as sorcery; witchcraft, they called it, or some such nonsense. At first, they were harmless. Paying the locals for stories that were falsehoods. The men began buying property and living among us. Still, we protected our secret. No one knew the last of all the world's magic remained with us, entrusted to us by the spirit world before they were forced off the earth. The men attracted unwanted attention from beings and things, dangerous things known to murder folks for their gifts. And unlike the men from the north, these creatures could smell magic; sense it.

"Murders began. These animals tortured our kin for days hoping to find the answers that the northerners asked. What was Obeah? Who among us still possessed the power of the ancient spirits? Magic of any kind was greatly feared. Man did not remember the older times when humans walked with faeries. Throughout the centuries, fact faded into folklore and then fantasy. And soon, no one remembered at all, except us and a minuscule amount of souls sprinkled around the globe."

"I do not understand any of this," Selina admitted.

"On the night you were born, the moon flamed an orange so bright, it appeared as if lava filled it. All of the doors to this world were wide open and connected to places long forgotten.

"The elders chose me to absorb their gifts. Your father objected, but it was when we found him dead, did I decide to accept my fate and yours."

"They killed him?"

"Yes, the murderers drained him of all of his blood, hoping he would tell them who possessed the gifts of the ancient ones. He took our identities to his grave.

"The plan had been for me to receive the last of all magic within my family. Take it and leave Martinique. I was the youngest and strongest. My pregnancy made me the best choice. The day you arrived, I absorbed the gifts of a dozen elders, but it was too much. My body could not sustain it, not even while carrying you. It threatened to end us both. The magic I newly inherited allowed me to communicate with the spirit world. The gods permitted me to cross worlds, leaving my body on Earth and leaving you an orphan. I left you with just enough magic to bring you here on this day."

"Wait a minute. You're dead too!" she yelled out, confused and unaware she'd been crying.

"The only way to save your life was to leave and change the fate of our family."

"You didn't save me. You left me alone. They found me alone in an orphanage in Dominica. Your family betrayed you and left me to die."

Selina didn't know where the rage inside her burned from, yet it did.

"Your identity needed to remain hidden even from you. My child, you will restore the nexus between worlds. The gods have chosen you. It is why we are here now. This is what kept me alive all this time."

"What do you mean?" Selina asked, frightened.

"By giving you what is rightfully yours, I will perish and take my place in the heavens."

"No!" Selina objected.

"Listen."

"No, I've only just met you. Let's just stay here. It's nice here," Selina pleaded.

"This is a gift. Today we celebrate your elevation. You are a lot stronger than I; smarter too." Elodie smiled.

"No. I don't want it. I didn't ask for it. Can't I refuse it and stay with you?"

"My child…"

"If this is what killed my dad and took my mom away from me, why would I want it? How could you want to give me this?"

"Time's almost up."

"I don't care." She sobbed, nearly hysterical. "You hand me a curse wrapped as a gift. No. I deny it."

"Augustus will die if you do not receive your birthright. If you refuse to step onto the road fate has chosen, he will be mutilated and suffer disfigurement. Does that comfort you?" Selina froze mid-breath. "He risked his life to bring you here."

"He said he cannot die."

"Right, but they can remove his limbs, blind him, burn him, leave him in such a state he will agonize for death. You must be there to prevent it."

Selina looked into Elodie's eyes for nearly ten wordless minutes. She studied every centimeter of her birth mother's face. And although she couldn't replicate the woman's fearlessness. She could do her damnedest to try. Quietly, acceptance seeped in.

"Many lives were lost for this day. You are loved. You are not some poor island orphan. You are a warrior, like me and my mom before. Do you hear me?"

"Yes," Selina answered.

"Now take my hands and let me give you what has been in our family for centuries. The transition will not be pleasant; prepare yourself. You will go through many phases. Do not be frightened. Remember, this will awaken the gifts of several of your ancestors. Each will feel unique to receive." Tears sparkled in Elodie's eyes. "I wish we had more time." She smiled with pride. "You must allow the spirit animals to pass through you. Do not let the sounds alarm you."

Selina nodded.

"I will be with you through all of it. For as long as the doors to your world are open." She hugged her daughter. "I am blessed to see you all grown up. It is my greatest joy." Elodie readied to begin.

"Wait. What was my name?"

"Laline (Lah-Leen). It means moon."

CHAPTER 13

THE BLOOD MOON

Kent's super flashlight revealed the cat first. Edha neglected to mention its size. The entire evening's search, the survivalist expected to encounter a mere house cat. To his surprise, the feline allegedly from hell was humongous, almost the size of a Canadian lynx. If he had not noticed the cat's long-haired bushy tail, he'd would've bet a bundle that it was in fact a lynx. But he knew those Canadian felines did not have long tails as the one before him.

Selina's head appeared *under* the cat. Fright seized Kent's senses. From the angle, even with the flashlight, the cat's torso loomed over Selina's head. He couldn't see it. The only conclusion was to assume the cat had hurt the girl. And he needed her alive. He needed to be the one to rescue her. He took a moment to imagine that story. He'd be a hero. He'd have the platform to promote his charities. God knew it wasn't greed, he reassured himself. This was bigger than a stupid wandering rich girl—one foolish enough to walk into an unknown timberland, alone with dangerous animals lurking behind every bush and branch. Right then, he decided to do whatever was necessary to get them both out of there alive. He aimed Edha's rifle at the feline's head. Kent had remarkable aim even though he hated hunting. He locked on to his target and pulled the trigger.

A loud shot rang out, but neither the woman nor the animal reacted. Suspicious, he aimed the rifle at a nearby tree for a close-range shot, knowing he didn't miss his target. He squeezed that trigger again, another loud pop exploded into the night, but no bullet exited the rifle.

"*BLANKS!*" he yelled to himself. "Crazy old bitch!" Edha gave him a rifle with blanks as ammunition. *Stupid cow,* he angrily thought again. For some reason, she wanted him to fail.

He returned his focus back to the original subjects. Drastic measures needed to be taken in order to get the girl away. If the sound of the shot did not spook the animal, another more aggressive course of action would be necessary. He switched the gun's position in his hands. He held the barrel in order to expose the butt of the rifle. When he got close, he swung the weapon backward intentionally to increase the speed of his forward swing like one would a baseball bat. The butt of the rifle connected ferociously to the cat's snout, nearly caving it in. The animal, too stunned to cry out, flew, crashing hard into nearby shrubbery.

Selina's eyes opened immediately.

"Where are you hurt?" Kent yelled. "Can you walk?" He held out his hand while his eyes surveyed the area for the cat's return. "Hurry before it comes back!"

"What did you do?" she whimpered. It'd been all she could muster. The journey back from her mother disoriented her. Kent did not reply. He grabbed her arm and yanked it forcefully enough to lift her nearly to her feet.

"I don't have time for this shit." He pulled at the same arm again, beginning to drag her.

"Wait. Stop!" She couldn't sense Augustus. She found it difficult to focus on any one thought. Her legs stiffened, then failed under her own weight. She could not prevent herself from being dragged.

"I knew you'd be trouble," Kent said more to himself. "Sometimes you can just tell." He continued to drag her until they reached a clearing. "I ain't gonna pull you the whole way." He stopped and let go of her arm. She fell to the ground. "Get UP!" he commanded. He surveyed her. No blood. No ripped clothing or injuries that he could see. If he had to guess, by her behavior, she exhibited the signs of an intoxicated person. It wouldn't be the first time a young adult went into the woods to get high. Angry at the idea of drug usage, he knelt down, cupping her face to examine her eyes. No dilated pupils. No signs of dehydration or inebriation. He stood up and looked away.

But she's been gone nearly two days, he thought to himself. Her skin felt warm. Selina's complexion did not exhibit evidence of exposure. Confused, he reached and gripped his own nose. As he suspected, it felt colder than his hands. He struggled to grasp why her temperature plagued him; it seemed an important clue to a mystery he was on the brink of solving.

"Alright now," he spoke at a much calmer tone. "It's time we head back." Fear trickled into his heart slowly at first. Of course, there was nothing to fear.

No one, not even law enforcement, will go into those woods under a moon like that.

The old woman's words repeated in his head. He hesitantly looked up and gasped in horror, aghast at what his eyes revealed to him.

The moon hung low. So low, Selina felt as though she could reach out and touch it from where she lay on the ground. Right before her very eyes, it transformed into a velvety crimson red. The moon, the wind, the sky, and stars beckoned to her. She felt an urgency. Suddenly, her left leg twitched; it involuntarily kicked up. The tingles and fizzes she felt earlier had been turned up to maximum. Elodie failed to mention how accepting her birthright would affect her.

The moonbeams awakened every cell in her body, changing it somehow. Reconfiguring her body inch by inch. One second, the neurons in her brain zapped her into unconsciousness; the next moment, the pressure in her chest mirrored the feeling of drowning. She didn't know how much longer her body could endure. She heard herself roar and snarl like a beast. This must be the spirit animals passing through. Selina braced herself for the worst.

CHAPTER 14

PECCAVISTI

K ent peeped over Selina, who had been moaning. Her legs twitched, yet that did not alarm him as much as her eyes, now appearing bloody and glowing.

"Holy shit," he exclaimed. "Selina, what the shit?" She let out a ghoulish groan that caused Kent to back away from her.

Long in his travels as a lover of Earth and a self-proclaimed child of the trees, he'd never seen such a hellish sight. Perhaps Edha got it wrong. Maybe the demon possessed the girl. And maybe, he never found the girl at all, he thought to himself. His entire slogan throughout his journey had been that of peace and discovery. Every living thing on this planet deserved a right to exist, he quoted relentlessly to his viewers. But this thing wearing Selina's body was not of this world. Kent Woodrow elected to kill it. Under the maddeningly bright blood moon, he began to sense his sanity slip. Maybe the old woman drugged him? He suspected, but he'd been searching for hours with no symptoms. This is what the old woman feared... So, he'd bring back its head. Surely, he'd still be a hero?

The gun proved useless. He patted his pockets for a more sufficient weapon. He found a small carving knife, nowhere near big enough to provide a fatal blow. Desperately, he searched the forest floor. He picked up a fallen branch. Quickly and quietly, he sharpened its edge.

The thing no longer Selina screamed—he crouched as low as his legs would let him. It sent another blood-freezing chill down his back, shrinking his balls.

Kent sharpened the makeshift spear he created. He initially planned to bludgeon the demon until it died and then cut off its head. The sounds coming from the creature disturbed him deeply. He never believed in spooks and goblins. Maybe Edha planted the demon theory into his mind, but she certainly could not have manipulated his eyes and ears. No way could anyone finagle this. It was real.

He crept over to where it lay, with a ghost-like silence. He avoided twigs, leaves, anything that would give his steps sound. The thing laid still. From afar, it just looked like a girl sleeping, but he *knew* better. He'd seen the glowing eyes and heard the snarls of a beast come from that body. Close now. He steadied his breathing despite his thundering heart booming in his throat. As he neared, tsunamis of terror wrecked his stomach to the point of almost vomiting. He raised the spear high, adjusting the grip for maximum descension. A sole bead of sweat swayed on the edge of his chin.

Do it. NOW!!! Kent's mind screamed. Kent closed his eyes, and his muscles made the decision to thrust the spear into the girl.

An unexpected collision occurred. Something lunged onto his face at such a speed, it knocked the man backward, causing both feet and hands to flair in the air desperately.

"Dear God," he panicked to himself as he soared. His head landed on a soft patch of earth with an echoing *thud,* yet to his revulsion, the unknown thing was still clutched to the flesh on his forehead. An animal, he concluded. He began to feel razor-sharp claws rip into his cheeks and right eye. Hot searing pain engulfed him as he felt his own blood run down his temple. *I'm gonna die out here!*

He scrambled to focus on anything other than his worsening wounds. Kent tried to remove the animal; it was superbly latched on his face closing in on his windpipe.

He reached out. Luck touched his fingertips. The spear had not fallen far from his grasp. Kent turned his entire body to the right, causing the attacker to lose its balance. The next second, he grabbed the animal, pushing it into the ground as he lifted himself. He realized the cat had returned. He only had a moment to glance at its deformed face from being hit by the butt of the rifle. The feline struggled under the man's weight but to no avail. Kent bared his knees down on the animal's ribs until he felt certain he heard a crack. The cat screamed out as much as it could until silenced by the man's hands around its throat. He removed one of his hands to pick up the spear nearby. He stared into the animal's bulging, broken eyes. Without hesitation, he lifted the spear once again to end the cat for good this time.

"Unhand him now!" Selina screamed from behind Kent. She could no longer sense Augustus in her mind. She attempted to connect to his in the way he taught her, but all she felt in return was fear and anguish.

A panicked Kent drove the spear into the cat's chest. Blood spilled from the cat as Selina watched her companion go limp. With minimal effort, she tossed the man to the other side of the clearing. Kent smacked into a tree and fell to the ground.

"What can I do?" she asked the feline. "Whatever you need. Tell me. Speak to my mind and I will do it!" The appearance of her friend, disfigured, beaten, and stabbed, broke her soul.

She yanked out the spear with shaky hands. "Tell me how to fix you," her voice cracked. Fresh tears streamed from her eyes freely. The cat did not answer her. She had taken too long to come into her gift. She was too late. Nothing could survive a pierced heart.

Selina had her back to the murderer. Kent decided to advance on her again. He crept up on her while he reached for his small blade. Even though she seemed completely normal, he had no doubt of the demon within. She about-faced when she felt him approaching.

"Why did you harm the cat?" she demanded. Kent remained silent. He clutched the small knife tighter. "Answer me!" she screamed. The wind picked up. If he didn't know any better, he could have sworn the wind brought her in front of him. Her legs never moved, yet with lightened speed, there she was. He turned to run. She violently seized him by the arm, causing him to cry out in pain. The girl twisted Kent around to face her. He spun fast and hard.

"My arm," he winced. "You dislocated my shoulder."

"You butchered it," she sobbed, "for nothing." Kent kept the blade firmly in his hand.

She waited for an explanation in disgust. As she looked at him, she imagined his throat tightening. She focused all her energy on suffocating the man with her mind. Kent gasped for breath.

"Demon," he choked. "Edha told me…" Selina focused even harder to silence him permanently. The man fell to the ground. Vomit erupted out of the man's nostrils as he asphyxiated. Selina looked away in repulsion, releasing him of her focus and energy.

Kent, still coughing and retching, scrambled to his feet. He ran away again. She let him.

"You will die, demon!" he screamed to her a distance away.

CHAPTER 15

THROUGH
THE DOORWAY

The body of the animal had ceased to function, yet the prisoner remained trapped. Pain from the hunter's tempestuous attack already began to fade. Yet more pressing difficulties arose. Its limbs ignored the commands to move. The cat's eyesight blurred until reaching total blindness. *How can I endure?* Augustus thought. He knew injury or even death to the cat's flesh would not restore him to his original self. He understood the risks of putting the figure in harm's way. Edha cautioned him many times, Charles, too.

"Your spirit is bonded to the animal: flesh, bones, and blood alike," he remembered. Edha warned, "You will remain with the beast through its dying death and decay; only until its bones are dust, may your spirit break free. And even then, the curse will remain as you live out a non-corporeal existence, never able to become whole again." She threatened to bury the cat alive if he kept escaping the grounds.

But what choice did he have? He, a cursed man with an exiguous possibility of freedom, had nothing to lose. Why wouldn't he risk his life for Selina? What life had he been living before she arrived? And if he succeeded in helping Selina escape safely, he would happily pay any price. The girl brought joy into his life. Happiness. Hope. He had to protect her with every living breath. And so, he did with valor and vigor, he thought as the cat's life force dwindled. In darkness and silence, Augustus wished he could've seen her one last time.

Selina half crawled; half ran back to the cat. She looked at the gaping hole in its chest. She repeated her earlier practices. She tried imagining the hole closed with her mind; it didn't.

"Elodie!" she cried into the night. "How do I undo this?"

She remembered what the cat said as she

looked up: "*A time when the earth, sun, and moon align so perfectly, a magic happens.*"

"I am Laline. Help me, please," she cried to the moon above. "Please help me undo what has happened to him." The night did not answer. "Open all doorways," she commanded. "Hear me now in this world and in the spirit world. Hear me everywhere my voice is carried."

She glanced down at the cat again. It protected her with its life. If it weren't for the cat, Edha would have locked her away or killed her. The journey that led her to her mom and her origin would never have happened. And then she thought of the man trapped in the cat, how his glacier-gray eyes warmed when looking at her. A glimpse of his face materialized in her mind. Augustus. The remembrance of him swelled her chest. *It will not be. This will not be the end of him*, she thought to herself with a vehement declaration.

A fire whirled around in the girl's abdomen. Strange sensations began pulsating outward, down her arms and legs. Something changed, like the magic in her body being conjured.

"I call unto those through the doorway of this night." Her hands burned.

"Help me!" she screamed desperately.

"UNDO WHAT WAS DONE TO HIM!" Her hands proceeded to glow.

"UNDO WHAT WAS DONE TO HIM!" she screamed at her highest possible volume.

"UNDO WHAT WAS DONE TO HIM!" The moon above her darkened from its former crimson color to a deep burgundy, nearly brown. Although dark, it hurt her eyes to look up at it, much like it would the sun. A concentrated burst of light beamed down on her. She raised both arms in the air to receive it.

"Yes!" she yelled. "Yes!" she repeated. "Help me help him, please." As she absorbed the beams, her whole body reacted, and for a moment, she couldn't breathe, as if the beams stopped her chest from inhaling. The girl's skin boiled from the inside out. But even if her body burst into flames, Selina vowed to bear it. All of it: the excruciating cranial pressure; the intense feeling of being cooked alive, she imagined, as if put inside of a microwave; the downpour of perspiration and tears that both stung and blinded her eyes. Determined more than ever, she suffered through.

Faces of souls, women mostly and some children, appeared to her mind during the true thick of it. Suddenly, the pain lessened. Hands brought her arms down from reaching up in the air; they redirected them to aim at the cat's dead body. Somehow, she felt her prayers answered. She pleaded for help, and many came.

It didn't matter if they were spirits, ghosts, or shadows reflecting ancient practices. For a second, she thought maybe these beings were hallucinations, figments of a desperate girl's imagination at a time when she felt the loneliest. But these faces smiled, and their hands took hold. The pain lessened, and all at once, she knew she would survive.

Light burned out of her body. A force lifted her off her feet. Embers scrambled everywhere.

UNDO WHAT WAS DONE TO HIM.

Power protruded out of her every orifice. Eyes, nostrils, ears, mouth, and rectum all burned. Just when she thought her eyes would pop out from the pressure, it stopped. She crashed to the ground, unconscious.

* * *

"Selina," a voice called to her softly. "Selina, are you okay?" Roused by the voice, she came to slowly. The moon appeared farther away, not as red as she remembered. The night sky did not provide as much light.

"Selina," the voice said again. She followed the sound; she could not believe her waking eyes. A naked man leered over her. "Selina, we need to leave here."

"Augustus," she half asked, half asserted. As a man? She could barely wrap her mind around it before darkness took her again.

Augustus carried Selina while sprinting through the woods. He nestled her head under his chin to keep it secure.

His bare human feet plowed through the piles of detritus on the forest floor. The branches scraped him as he soared by, leaving small cuts on his bare skin. Augustus ran harder, faster, gulping in tornadoes of air for his burning lungs. Every muscle was alive with both fear and disbelief. Terror outweighed all other thoughts and feelings. He ran as if a different version of reality chased him: An alternate series of events that would undoubtedly undo his current freedom. The man quickened his pace even faster. He ran until his legs could no longer support the weight of the two of them. He stopped abruptly before they completely gave out on him. Augustus placed Selina gently on a bed of umbrageous bluegrass before collapsing beside her.

* * *

A cloud of purple butterflies fluttered on the gentle wind of a warm afternoon. Dozens of large, hand-sized creatures swayed all around Augustus. A closer look revealed the very outer end of their wings appeared to be wrapped in black lace. Inside the lace, its wings bore a rich purple sheen color with white dots. Those butterflies brought a joy to his heart that felt strange. Excitedly perplexed, he extended his arm outward, in hopes that one of the winged beauties embrace him in touch; none did. Disappointed, he began to look beyond the butterflies. Tall beech trees stood on both sides of a beaten walking path—a path he'd swore he walked before many times. Familiarity pangs jabbed at him. It wasn't until his nostrils filled with oak did he recognize he'd been to this place.

"The purple emperor," he heard a voice say. A voice that he knew.

"Abigail!" He whisked around to see her. His sister stood a distance away, her image shadowy, like a projection. "Abigail," he repeated louder.

"These are the only butterflies that do not feed on flowers. They feed on rotting flesh," she said, clearly, into his mind. Questions flooded his head. *Where are the others? How long has it been?* Abigail's screams remained an unshakable source of despair during his imprisonment, like a demon under the bed of his memories.

"Abigail, come closer. I'm free!" he yelled to the image. "She broke my chains, Sister."

The aura of his sister drifted farther away. He closed his eyes tightly, hoping to see her in his mind. She did not appear.

"You were gone a very long time. None of your kin remains. Our bits and bones are sprinkled about the earth under your feet. We have left this world."

His heart ached, weighed down with dread. He long feared his family dead. He could not bear a confirmation of this sort.

"Brother."

"Abigail."

"What is left of us lives in the heart of our home. The lakes, trees, rivers, and leaves; and every creature in between." Augustus opened his eyes at the haze of butterflies surrounding him. Some of the winged insects appeared to have been looking straight at him. A single tear welled up in his eye. "What is left of me," Abigail continued, "lives in the heart of my beloved."

"Jackson?" he questioned, baffled by her absurdity. Wasn't he also a loved one?

"Yes, Brother, he lives still, and you must go to him."

"Abigail, I cannot bear to think of the fate you suffered." He closed his eyes once more. "Many innocents paid for the crime of our hubris. Most of all, you, dear sister.

"Free Jackson. When the news of your escape spreads, he will be ended."

Augustus paused in thought. She loved Jackson beyond her years of life. For a second, he was jealous, but something changed. The butterflies scattered away. He knew he was alone. Light shining from somewhere else increased. He could not hold himself there.

"Abigail! Abigail!" he cried out, frantic. "I will go to him. I will find him."

Behind his closed eyes, he heard Selina groan in pain, and his heart wept. He knew it meant he was never with his departed sister. And he will never be again.

CHAPTER 16

ALCHEMY AND APPARATUSES

"Oh my," Selina spoke shyly. "You're not a cat anymore. You're a very naked man." She laughed, averting her eyes awkwardly. Augustus jerked his right index finger toward his chest and zapped clothes on his body.

The freed prisoner and his liberator looked at each other for a few moments. The formerly naked man now clothed, dressed in a seaweed-green tunic with tattered and shipwrecked-looking pants bearing the same color. To Selina, his outfit looked like a generic elf costume found in any discount store around Halloween.

"It's funny," Selina said uneasily, "because I always say, '*What the Frock*' and you're wearing a frock." Augustus stared back, confused.

"My attire?" he asked. "Is it not suitable?" His eyes begged for her approval. Augustus's body language exuded a strong need for acceptance. Although taller than her, he kept his head bowed, sights fixed on his own feet. There was undoubtedly a difference in culture.

She often used humor in uneasy situations. In this case, her teasing *felt* mean. *He is not of this time,* she reminded herself. She opted to grant him her pleasure, knowing it would make him happy to have achieved it.

"It's perfect for now," she answered softly. "If we ever leave this forest, you might want to blend in, as not to draw attention."

"I understand," he affirmed happily. "Where is it that you wish to go?"

"I want to get to the next town over, call my d-d..." She stammered to address Brett as her dad after she learned of her biological father's sacrifice. "My adopted parents." She turned her phone back on.

"We are in the next province; it is not far enough. Kent is definitely going to go back and tell the others of what took place." The iPhone turned on without issue. Luckily, it survived the battles from the night before.

"It says we're in the Prairie Province."

"I didn't hear anything."

"What?"

"You said, *it said,* suggesting the device in your hand can speak."

"Right, I meant it *read.*" She turned the phone over. He looked at it briefly, then resumed smiling at her.

"At the cabin, people used those apparatuses for directions. It occupies a built-in compass," he spoke, unsure of the correct words to use. "It shows where you are? A find my phone?" He spoke as both a question and a statement.

Rats, she thought.

"You frowned. Did I upset you?"

"No, you're right." She turned her phone off again. "This *apparatus,* aka iPhone, does have a tracker. They probably know where we are now."

"Then we must go," Augustus said hastily.

"We have no money. My credit cards, debit cards, Uber, everything I have can be tracked," She sighed. "I left my backpack with all our food. We certainly cannot walk to New York."

"I met a man on my journey, kin to my party of nine. He taught me how to travel through water, wood, and rock. We can try it, but it took nearly a month for me to learn."

"I don't have a month to learn it," Selina barked. "They have cars. They can find us in under a day."

"Is it just currency we lack?" Augustus's features lit up. He knelt to the ground and aggressively dug his hands deep in the tough October soil. Baffled by his actions, she inched away from him.

"Nearer! I need you closer to me." He strained. As he struggled, his arms sunk lower into the dirt. She stepped closer than she had been previously to the gentleman who was up to his armpits in the ground.

"What are you doing?" she asked, mystified by his actions.

He pulled out two gold bars. One in each hand.

"How did you?"

"I met an alchemist named Luciano, from Portugal. He'd been the first to join Jackson and me." He smiled. "This country mines gold, among other metals and minerals."

"So, the ground gave you gold?" Selina asked sarcastically.

"No. It's more than that. Perhaps I will explain the art of magic and alchemy to you at a later time." He smiled again, incredibly pleased with himself. "Will this suffice?"

"Damn straight," Selina said, slapping her companion on his back as she began to walk ahead. Augustus stood in place, confused. The girl looked back. "That means great work. Thank you!"

Augustus smiled effulgently. She could not help but notice the more handsome he appeared when happy.

They hailed the first vehicle that appeared once the two reached a road. Immediately, they asked if he could transport them to New York. The sandy-haired, portly, middle-aged man pouted in his four-door pickup truck.

"As much as I'd like to help strangers, that's too big of a deed to do." He grimaced as if hating to say no. "I can drive you to my uncle. He flies a regional cargo jet. If you have another one of those bars, I'm sure he'll take you. You'll be in New York by tomorrow."

"He's a pilot?" Selina asked.

"Has he acquired his own vessel?" Augustus interrupted. The driver shot a sideways glance to Selina, confused.

"I don't know what you folks are mixed up in. Maybe helping you is not a good idea."

"We are running away together," Selina said quickly. "Our families didn't want us together," she begged. "New York is best for both of us."

The driver relaxed a bit. Forbidden love seemed to be a topic he understood.

"Are you sure you guys want to just up and leave your families? You both look pretty young."

Augustus snatched Selina's hand.

"This woman rescued my heart from a terrible misery. I *will* follow her anywhere in this world and beyond."

"Wow, that was intense." He sighed. "Young love usually is," he chuckled. "Call me Biff."

"Laline," Selina introduced, "and this is Gus—short for Gustavo." She saw the confused look on her companion's face when she did not give their real names. She hoped the driver did not sense her deception.

"Well, okay." Biff smiled. "Hop on in. It's about an hour or so away."

The two passengers climbed in the back. Augustus grabbed hold of her arm and squeezed it. She sensed his nervousness. It might be his first time in a pickup truck, or any truck for that matter. She wished their mental link hadn't severed. He dropped her hand and clutched both sides of her face. Their foreheads touched.

"Meh-Mon," he said to her mind. Selina smiled. She sought his hand to hold it. *"This is all so strange. The world changed a lot from when I walked its roads. I'm afraid I'm inept."*

"It's an adjustment," she replied to his mind. *"You are far more capable than you were a day ago."*

"I fear my maladroit behavior embarrasses you. It is not my intention. I apologize." Augustus's statement bore genuine sincerity. She observed a fleck of green in his otherwise silver-gray eyes. It dawned on her that this had been the first time she ever *really* looked into them. The previous encounters between them took place in a dream state. Suddenly, the magnitude of their situation inundated her. Last night, the man whose eyes

she found herself immersed in wasn't a man at all. He was a *cat!*

Bizarre, she thought, but then bizarre failed to define all that occurred. She met Elodie and came to know of her true heritage, the gifts her blood possessed. *The power…*

"You are troubled." Augustus sensed. He illustrated deep concern and almost sorrow on his face.

"How romantic!" Biff screamed from the front seat. "You two haven't stopped looking at each other since you got in." He laughed. "It's not creepy at all… Well, it sorta is." Selina turned and noticed the driver leering at them in his rearview mirror.

Biff's uncle Joey happily accepted the payment in exchange for secret transport. Luckily, he'd already been assigned a New York manifest scheduled for that evening. The couple only need wait 'til then.

* * *

"My sister fell in love with a mortal, human city dweller. Her love transformed him. This is rare. The males of my people amassed value before the elders permitted any unions. Our people never needed money, so value, in this case, meant skill, trade, or ability," Augustus said, hunched inside the cargo compartment of Joey's commercial plane. Selina sat beside him, hugging her knees. Around them were boxes of various shapes and sizes, envelopes too.

"And the lady in waiting, what is her task?" Selina asked.

"She chooses. In my time, if you selected me to be yours, I must deem myself worthy to the elders."

"How?"

"The men went off to find uninhabited lands, built shelters, dams, gardens, anything to prove he could take care of his family."

"Wow," she sighed heavily, "our times are very different." A long silence occurred. "So, how did you deem yourself worthy?" she finally asked.

"Unfortunately, I was not selected. None of the women in my village chose me."

"That's nonsense!" she exclaimed.

"At the time of her maturation, my mother chose three potential husbands: my father among them. To prove himself, Tarquin, my father, embarked on a journey of discovery. During the story, he admitted many times his ignorance. The man wandered around baffled and bewildered, completely clueless as to how he planned to demonstrate himself worthy. Three days later, he encountered an elderly man crippled and writing in pain. The white-haired hunchback fellow veered deep into the country in search of an herb rumored to relieve the ache of old age. In exchange for my father's knowledge of pain-relieving plants, the gentleman taught him how to read and write."

"He couldn't read?" Selina asked, surprised.

"My people practiced the ancient language of where we lived. The man taught my father English, the common tongue of the city dwellers.

"It's a long story. To end it quickly: My mum chose him. Together they built a small school where she taught us the fundamentals: reading and writing. My dad kept his interest in medicine. He assembled a hut for his herbs. Their union advanced generations after them in both science and language. I couldn't offer a bride anything similar." He turned his gaze toward the small oval window of the aircraft.

"Talk about pressure," she stated plainly. Augustus remained focused on the view outside of the window.

"We are lowering," he observed.

"We will be landing shortly. Welcome to New York City," they heard the pilot announce.

"Now's the time to change," she whispered.

He zapped himself again. He wore Selina's exact look—the jeans, boots, and jacket—however, he kept the color of seaweed-green.

"You have got to teach me that," she chuckled. "Well, at least you are consistent with the green."

"Is it not suitable?" he panicked. "I am exactly as you are."

She surveyed his clothing once again. If she squinted, Augustus reminded her of an Irish Army Cadet, without the hat.

"You are perfect," she said finally, and she meant it.

CHAPTER 17

KENT'S RETURN

Charles sat across from Edha at her dining room table. The tea in both cups still steamed amongst an array of untouched breakfast delights; neither of them had much of an appetite.

"The sun rises without rays," Charles said somberly.

"Magic," she whispered. "But whose?"

A large crash outside her door, followed by sporadic slow thumps, seized both of their attention. Edha turned the knob on her front door, and it flew open.

"You sent me out there with blanks." Kent barged into the doors of Edha's cabin, practically crawling from exhaustion.

"What folly is this?" Charles demanded. As the two occupants approached their uninvited guest, his stench preceded him. Edha immediately smelled vomit on the man. In addition, Kent emitted a sour musky odor from sweat and various other bodily secretions. The unpleasant smell did not alarm Charles as much as the man's wounds did. The jagged, deep slashes on the explorer's face were in dire need of medical attention. Charles's concern grew at the sight of Kent's right eye, which was also cut and crusted over with blood. "I'm calling Ted and Ramón," Charles said, rushing to his cellular phone.

"Did the cat do this?" Edha asked, frantic. "What of the girl?"

"You sent me in there *knowing* what she was, knowing what she'd do!" Kent rambled, spitting as he spoke and on the verge of collapse. "You knew and sent me out there to *rescue* her anyway."

"What of the cat?" Edha asked again louder. Kent spiraled towards the floor, unable to keep any portions of himself upright. He fell into her reluctant arms. She lowered him flat on the ground. "What happened?" she asked aggressively.

"I stabbed it in the fucking chest," he said with much effort. "I killed the cat and left the demon alive."

"What does that mean? Explain!" Edha ordered, but it was no use. Kent succumbed to his exhaustion.

"Hola," Dr. Ramón Ferrero, one of the two doctors, said as he crossed the threshold of Edha's open door.

"Charles, we're here," Dr. Tedward Dawson, the other doctor, announced loudly before entering. "We're walking in now. I hope everyone is decent."

"¡Hijole!" Ramón shrieked in a thick Spanish accent, shocked by Kent's injuries. "Esta herido!" That man is badly injured.

"We cannot treat him here. He needs fluids and stitches now!" Tedward echoed.

Edha recruited Tedward and Ramón just as they finished their intern year at the University Hospital several years back. Both men possessed distinctive traits. Ramon, although born in Canada, his parents migrated from Argentina. She defined him as tall, dark hair, exotically handsome, highly intelligent, and very sociable. A perfect addition to her staff.

En Tutum's single female guests were all wealthy and powerful. They usually came to relish in Canada's magnificent rustic sceneries from the windows of their mansion-styled cabins. The company of Dr. Ramon Ferrero added the needed touch of charm and fantasy to an otherwise dream excursion.

Dr. Tedward Dawson, a London native, proved a perfect contrast to Ramón with ocean-blue eyes and golden-blonde hair. He was also tall, traditionally handsome yet bougie, not as social, pompous, and a bit of a know-it-all. The gentlemen visitors loved him best. Both doctors lived on the grounds to respond to emergent situations, such as Kent's current one, quickly.

She watched them load Kent's unconscious body into their private ambulance with incredible haste.

"Wait," Edha said. "I found these in his things." She held out her hand.

"Drugs?" Ramón asked, running to the driver's seat of the truck

"Yes, very similar." Edha forced herself to frown. "Hallucinogens."

"Well, that explains everything," Tedward exclaimed while preparing Kent for transport. "Those are illegal out here."

"I'm sure he didn't know," she said to the doctors, trying her hardest to sound caring and protective. "Mr. Woodrow is quite out of his mind at the present. He should be sedated immediately. It is the best and only treatment to keep him comfortable." Both men nodded in agreement. She knew if he gained consciousness, they'd put him right back out.

"Hallucinogens?" Charles questioned Edha when she returned from outside. "Is that how you intend to silence him?"

"Kent is suffering from exhaustion, dehydration. Maybe he lost a lot of blood, too, who knows?" she answered.

"The man suffered a mauling, Edha. No amount of rest will remedy that face," Charles said. "Sedation will not change his account of events."

"He is of small concern to me. He used *Demon* to describe the girl," she stated, perplexed. "He said, '*I killed the cat but left the demon alive!*'"

"It appears the girl has completed the ascension."

"There hasn't been an ascension since the nine were imprisoned. It does not make sense."

"But there is also an unraveling in your heart, woman, the same in mine. You know what I know."

"It cannot be!" she muttered, barely audible.

"The girl made us feel uneasy from the start, something about her," he said faster and with great emphasis. "She bared the mark of Obeah. We saw it on her hand, Edha."

"Many babies from that part of the world are given that mark when they are born. It is not confirmation."

"What of the hunter, is HE NOT confirmation?"

"We must find the cat's body. We must confirm that the prisoner is still captive. Even if an ascension took place, she'd be ignorant to the full scope of her power. She couldn't have released Augustus."

"Too many ifs," Charles asserted. "We should caution the other sites, tell them a freer is among us and may try to release more of the nine."

"Utter lunacy," Edha said accusingly. "We do not even know if one was freed. Why rush to the pits of hell, needlessly?"

"You signed a blood oath. We both swore on pain of death to keep the cat a cat, alive and imprisoned."

"I know the story, Charles. I lived it. You needn't remind me of what's at stake."

"You may have your little charms and glamor illusions, but you are not preternatural. Against them, you are not an opponent. You are a bug. Just do what was instructed for once." Charles spoke sharply as he walked towards the exit.

"Father Time has also done away with your courage, old man," Edha spewed in response, but Charles was gone. Soon, her dining room resumed its quaint and quiet ambiance as normal, allowing her mind to fill with gnawing questions.

Why would Kent call Selina a demon? How could she have missed the girl's magical presence? How did the cat know? All inquiries, no answers.

Edha fulfilled her blood oath as far as she was concerned. She held her post as ward. She built walls, traps, and hired armed guards—all to keep the animal trapped on the premises. In truth, she grew tired. And come what may, her soul was ready.

CHAPTER 18

THE APRĪCŌRUM

E dha lied in bed listening to her service staff dispose of the breakfast no one touched. She focused on the clinking sounds of the plates being scraped and the lighthearted greetings between her workers.

Tried as she might, her mind prevented her from revisiting the Bazaar. Instead, memory lane led her to a sad moment. The day her dad took her away.

Edha was the bastard daughter of a wealthy Persian visitor Behman Esfandiari. Mr. Esfandiari came to collect Edha on her thirteenth birthday. He paid a rather generous dowry to his former mistress (her mother, Anahitha) for her blessing. He promised an education for his daughter, an acknowledgment of paternity, and claims to his inheritance. He argued he could not bear to watch his blood kin live like a common rat scraping for change any longer. Despite Anahitha's reservations, she accepted the money in exchange for her daughter.

He could offer her a better life, better status. Edha could marry well, Anahitha must have thought, Edha supposed, even though her mind gnawed and knotted with doubts. The next morning, he whisked his daughter away from everything and on to Iran, called Persia at the time. The three-story Esfandiari property consisted of large stone walls and stained-glass windows. Never had her eyes witnessed such a magnificent display of wealth. Inside were mosaic floors; sophisticated paintings decorated the walls. Compared to the straw-filled sack she slept on with her mom back in Tajikistan, she felt like royalty, however short-lived.

Soon after her arrival, four female servants scrubbed Edha's skin nearly raw. She remembered her hair yanked, twisted, and pinned all in preparation to meet the matriarch of her father's family: the great-grandmother Faja.

"You do not have the *gift* of our blood," Faja said with an obvious tinge of disappointment. "We can teach you the ways of our women, but you will not rise above novice." Ashamed by the woman's words, she looked away teary-eyed.

"Maybe your daughter will have it," the great-grandmother said, "but you, you're just another mouth to feed."

As the months passed, Edha learned charm, persuasion, seduction, dance, and glamour. Although Edha absorbed each skill with full adaption, she never received as much as a glance from the Esfandiari elders again. While there, she learned her dad fathered many children and always presented the females to Faja on their thirteenth birthday. It seemed an odd tradition, one she'd never know the answer to. Instead, they entrusted Edha to her father's third wife, Minu (Mee-New), a woman also outcasted by the matriarchs for not yet producing any children.

Rumors of the nine men grew. An entire imperial palace collapsed into the ground in Japan. Witnesses swore the mouth of hell opened up to swallow it whole. Two thousand five hundred people died, and Masayori claimed responsibility. He valued fear above all else.

And with that, fear spread easily. Whispers of witchcraft floated through the air like spirits haunting their village. Soon, all magical beings were deemed dangerous; too dangerous to remain alive. People sanctioned public murder for the sake of their own safety.

Two months shy of her fourteenth birthday, a mob of residents stampeded the courtyard of their grandiose home. Armed with stones, torches, and anything else fashioned as a weapon, the villagers—people that Edha knew and recognized—forced themselves in and dragged her family out. Nearly the entire line of Esfandiari women dragged out of the home like animals as their men stood by helpless, Edha's father included.

Faja screamed into the maddening mob before they set her ablaze. The crowd stoned Faja's daughters before burning them too. Of the Esfandiari women, only Minu and Edha was spared. She attributed their mercy to the gossiping servants who called Edha a *dud*. And Minu, who was of no relation.

Minu grabbed three small bags already filled with jewels. Knowing in her heart this day would come, she luckily had an escape already planned out. She collected Edha and slipped into the secret corridor, leading them outside away from the frenzied crowd. They fled on two camels. Minu, dressed in her husband's Shalvah and Jameh. The two escaped posing as a lad and his young bride. They fled to Turkey.

* * *

Five years later, near Edha's eighteenth birthday, a dark stranger appeared at their door. By then, she and Minu had reached Bulgaria and settled in a fishing town bordering the black sea.

Rafik, a Moroccan native, a Moor, and a member of the Aprīcōrum, arrived at their antiquated home. The handsome bearded man towered over Edha. He stood a full six inches higher than her 5'6" height, although, in his white and golden turban, he appeared much taller. He requested Edha's presence respectfully. Before meeting him, she did not know of the Aprīcōrum's existence. Confounded by her unawareness, he decided to sit Edha down and start from the very beginning.

"The spirit world is an astral realm between this world and the heavens," Rafik explained. "Before Earth could sustain mortal life, gods inhabited it. Gods and demons, to be exact. Imagine this planet crawling with entities that thrived in darkness, with no need of warmth, air, or water."

Edha shuddered at the thought.

"When life began, both were driven off Earth to the spirit world. Although, the demons returned every so often to eat human souls, corrupt them with darkness and black magic. The gods were not pleased. The Aprīcōrum were apostles ordained by the Light God, holder of the eternal flame.

"Legend says the deity gifted twelve humans with a portion of his own magic to protect Earth from demons and the humans who were tainted by them. As a reward, all fallen acolytes are granted entry into the spirit world for an eternity of bliss."

"Are you one of the twelve?

"Yes. There are always only twelve. When one dies, the magic chooses another. It was my father before me and my grandmother before him," he answered patiently. "We exist to stop dark magic, also, the dark hearts that yield magic and will it to harm others."

"Like the nine?"

He nodded. "Yes. My people vanquished the nine," he announced proudly.

"Murdered?" Edha asked.

"Worse." He smiled deviously. "Cursed."

"How were you able to subdue such a mighty group of men?"

"One of them came to us." He smiled again. "Not all of their souls were evil."

"What is it that you want from me? Why have you tracked me here? I am not a carrier of magic."

"You come from a powerful and dangerous bloodline. We needed confirmation, more than what a servant could testify."

"And now?"

"Now, I wish you to accompany me back home so that I may ask permission to wed you."

Edha blushed. "You can stop running. Walk in the light with me. Be my bride."

Their union never took place. Rafik was murdered within months of them arriving at his home in Lithuania, burned alive in an explosion derived from dark magic. The killer paid for his crime, but justice did nothing to lessen Edha's broken heart. Every time she thought of a place as home, tragedy struck, spoiling it. His bredren, the other eleven followers, was occupied with a new crisis that would change life for everyone—a superterrestrial event prophesied to damage the bridge linking the spirit world to Earth. A celestial rift threatened to trap all magical beings in either place. The Aprīcōrum decided to leave rather than remain on Earth.

The *see-ers* foresaw a sustainable answer as long as no magic existed. With that forecast, all magical beings were forced to leave with the Aprīcōrum or die.

This decision was well-liked for the most part, but there were those that opposed it. Pregnancies were hidden. Children stashed away. Not everyone wanted to leave their home for the unknown.

The Aprīcōrum entrusted Earth to its scholars. What need for magical healers when doctors soon tended to the sick and ailing. Monarchs led the laws and enforced order. Democracy and education seemed a better way for humans to thrive. With magic gone, there was no longer a need to protect Earth.

A few non-magical Stuarts were chosen as wards, Edha included. She swore to protect her prisoner with her entire life, and the reward would be success, fame, beauty—anything beyond all she could ever imagine. Her life prior was infested by poverty and loss. This seemed a fitting gift. Yet years turned into decades, decades merged into centuries, and soon magical beings were forgotten entirely, including the nine in prison.

Edha realized two things: Magic survived, despite their strongest efforts. And if the nine were unleashed on this world again, there was no Aprīcōrum to stop them.

* * *

~ The Next Day ~

"Our search crew discovered a backpack belonging to your missing guest, Ms. Horton," Deputy Sheriff Fox reported. "We also found multiple blood-spatter patterns all over the surrounding area."

"What's that?" Edha asked.

"The K9s dug up a bloody spear hidden in the dirt. It might be the weapon responsible for the pools of blood out there."

"So, dogs digging in the dirt is a part of your case?" Edha pompously stated. "And finding sticks no less?"

"I beg your pardon! We work with Belgian Shepherds, the smartest, most dedicated military animals," the deputy spouted agitatedly. "Don't you think they'd know the difference between day-old blood and month-old?" He stared at Edha, awaiting an answer. None came. "You know what? This is a police matter, which means it's confidential. Good day, madam." Fox proceeded to storm out of Edha's dining room toward the front door.

Charles shot Edha a displeasing look.

"Deputy Fox," Charles called out as he ran down the officer. "I must apologize deeply for my co-owner's perversity." The officer returned his own angry glance. "How about you and your team set up operations right here in two of our biggest cabins?"

"Mr. Elkins, that's very generous, but police officers—me included—cannot accept gifts or bribes; it's unethical."

"Nonsense. I know it's a long drive, at least a few hours away from the sheriff's office. It will present as a hardship for your officers eventually."

"It does sound amazing, but my superiors will never go for that," Fox said regrettably.

"Leave that to me. Go home. Pack a bag for a few days. I guarantee you will get the call tonight." Fox smiled, unable to contain his excitement.

"I couldn't ever afford a place like this," Fox admitted. "I appreciate your efforts, whatever the outcome."

"I will personally assure you and your team receive the full experience of En Tutum; off duty, of course," Charles promised. "Hurry back now and wait for the call." Charles and Edha watched the young deputy exit the front door with an extra spring in his step. "You must adjust that imperious attitude," Charles said to Edha, still watching Deputy Fox.

"You want them all here, in our best suites?" she asked, appalled. "Who's going to pay for that?"

"You will. It will be your personal responsibility to adhere to their every need."

"Preposterous!" Edha scowled. "I will do no such task."

"Yes. You will," Charles stressed. "The happier we keep them, the more we can control this investigation." Edha sneered. "We need their help, like it or not." Edha continued to display a hateful expression.

"And despite your reservations, it is time to alert the others," Charles continued.

Edha examined Charles's smug look. She imagined slapping him right across the face. He walked off, leaving her alone as he always did when they disagreed. Her frustration rose into fury. She obviously did not want to make the call. She had no answers. She didn't know if the prisoner remained captive in the cat's body. She didn't know if the girl escaped; for her information, both could be dead and buried. Of course, she did not want to cause alarm needlessly.

Edha sat at her dining room table. The hot tea in her cup swirled smells of eucalyptus up her nose

Perhaps we need the cops' help, she thought to herself. Kent remained sedated and unhelpful to her. The surgeon stated that he might lose sight in the eye that was infected. "How did things go so wrong so fast?" she asked herself.

The girl will know every answer, she concluded. She must increase the search for her. And then, suddenly, she decided to make Selina the most wanted woman in Canada.

CHAPTER 19

THE WILLOW TREE

The cemented ground felt strange to walk on. The asphalt roads, black rubbery streets, and massively tall buildings with mirrored walls overwhelmed Augustus. The noise accosted him first. Shortly after they exited the aircraft, the deafening sounds hit him all at once. Drivers incessantly honking their vehicles in the streets, all while screaming out of the window: "Hurry up, move!" People walked everywhere, uncomfortably close to one another, some talking loudly into their apparatuses. No one had any regard for the other. They all walked as if they had the street to themselves; everyone pressed for time with brittle patience.

Suffocating smog invaded his fresh lungs. Smoke emanated from the exhaust pipes of several double-parked delivery vehicles. The air also reeked of burning food. He looked to the far-left corner of the street and noticed a peanut vendor roasting nuts; a thickened cloud of smoke accompanied him. Across the street, an empanada truck seared fresh beef to its customers. Finally, to the very far right stood a halal cart that read: *Serving the very best lamb and rice this side of Columbus Circle.*

"Oh dear," he gasped quietly to himself. His chest tightened. The constant movement of midday on Broadway left him feeling closed in. This cold, gray place, nothing like *En Tutum* where he'd been held captive. Not so much as a tree as far as his eyes wandered. Not one blade of grass he could sense. He'd never been this far away from his comforts. In his entire existence as both man and beast, there was nary a day he did not have greenery among his steps. He panicked. He never wanted to be more invisible in his life. *What happened to this world?* he pondered. And just for a nanosecond, he missed Canada. He missed strolling around the grounds and the silence of the forest. Afraid he may appear weak to Selina, he closed his eyes and tried to keep up as best he could. He collided hard with a Korean businessman.

"Open your eyes!" the man yelled.

"Eyes in front, you idiot!" Another man wearing a hard hat and yellow reflective gear scowled.

"Keep moving, asshole!" Selina shouted, startling Augustus too. She clutched his arm as he stood in the middle of Broadway, trembling.

"It's maddening," he said to her mind. "Pure chaos. I can barely stand the noise. The smells. What is this hell?"

Selina had been so used to the aroma it was as if she developed an immunity. Yes, the people were loud. New York traffic was infamously terrible.

Also, the air *was* thick with smog. Ubers, taxis, noncommercial cars, delivery trucks, and mail trucks all emitted smoke into the atmosphere. Okay, she got it. But they couldn't stop here; they must keep moving, and she needed to convince him of that now before they were spotted.

Although she grasped him loosely, she still observed his body vibrate with terror. And she tried to imagine his plight once again.

"Keep focused on me. We will be indoors soon, I…" Before her words provided their intended comfort, he zipped out of her hold easily and fled at such a speed, she hardly saw a green blur. "Okay," she said to the oblivious New Yorkers walking by, "apparently, he's also the fucking Flash."

* * *

His mind's eye delivered him to Morning Side Park. He ran upon the paved road until he reached a large pond. Across the pond, near a bed of large rocks, stood a twenty-foot willow tree of the weeping variety. At risk of discovery, he used a small amount of his magic to jolt himself underneath its swaying vine-like branches. He placed his face up against the tree bark. The tree did its best to console Augustus. The sage-colored, lance-shaped leaves cascading downward concealed him from any potential outside onlookers. His own personal veil.

Acknowledging that fact, he relaxed. He allowed the surrounding sounds of the park to soothe him. He observed the local geese glide about the pond happily. And although hidden from sight, he sensed the many turtles hibernating on the pond floor. Nearby, a woodland songbird, the brown creeper, hopped about its way merrily. His entire body unclenched, releasing the tension.

As restored to his natural state, he sensed a problem in the tree. He hugged it, placing his palms on opposite sides of its bark. Within seconds, he identified the illness. Augustus smiled, knowing his specific gift offered a lifesaving remedy.

"I can help you, old gal," he said aloud. He instructed his magic to seep inside, slowly covering both the inner and outer layers, not leaving so much as a splinter untreated. Augustus pushed further, past the trunk and into the soil, where the roots of the tree were beginning to rot. His powers wrapped around the rotted areas of the root, hardening it, encouraging it to reinforce itself by growing in diameter. As a result, the roots dug deeper into the earth until it reached a much more stable location, a healthier drier place not conducive to deterioration from outside factors. A thought suddenly occurred to him: *What if the tree lured me?* It compelled his fleeing steps to its direction. Maybe on a subconscious level, a mere inch or two beyond his awareness, he felt its duress. He wondered how long it waited for someone to understand its cries. Where he came from, the people were much more in tune with the trees around them.

Gratitude permeated from the willow. And for a few seconds, he allowed himself to enjoy a task well done. He did it alone, without help, without needing to be near a more powerful being. An unexpected tear rolled down his cheek. He wiped it away quickly. A second drop fell fast, barely touching his face at all before it shattered on his jacket. The third one, he didn't bother to wipe. Feelings of sadness overtook him. Healing the willow tree reminded him of the first time he'd ever used his gift. Barely a teenager then, his younger self held the fleeting gift of a mother's love, a father's protection, a whole family, and community support. He thought of his sister Abigail. His sorrow increased. Reluctantly, Augustus began to sob loudly. All of them were dead. He had been left alone in a world that was changed. He worried about his ability to adapt to it.

How long had it been? Decades? A century? More? At what point did the forests diminish? And how was it reduced to the cold gray and black horror that was New York City? Was he the very last forest dweller? The thought made him quiver as his sobs grew stronger, nearly buckling him. He cross-clutched his midsection tightly, hoping his gasps would subside soon. In all, it felt good to *cry*. It felt appropriate. In the years he walked as a cat when sorrow engulfed him, he merely carried it along. Unable to release it. Unable to mourn. Unable to live. He did not belong in this time.

* * *

Selina appeared dramatically as if out of thin air. She found her companion, hunched over, crying hysterically. She prepared to scold him for running off the way he did and explain how frightened she became when she thought him lost in a place like New York City. One look at him melted away her anger.

She pulled Augustus into her arms forcefully. He did not resist.

"It's okay," she whispered. "You're okay." She held him tighter, seemingly holding him up. He clung to her, burying his face in the cusp of where the neck meets the shoulder. She cradled him closely until his sobs subsided.

"I've never cried like that," his mind said to hers. *"I'm ashamed."*

"I cry like that all the time," she replied untruthfully. "We're human; it happens." She began to stroke his hair, lightly grazing the back rims of his ears with her fingernails. Her touch created tingle trails all throughout his scalp. Goosebumps erupted down his back. *Remarkable.* He thought of how much her presence soothed him. Moments prior, he bawled almost to the point of retching.

The sorrow, grief, and guilt all tied his heart in knots. And a moment with her, all traces of his sadness faded. *Surely this is some form of bewitchment,* he guessed. How did she manage to end his suffering without a twinkle of magic? Slowly, he removed his arms from around her waist.

"Why did you run?" Selina asked aloud.

"The tree called me here."

"I thought you couldn't take all the people and noises; I probably should've cautioned you. It is intense."

"I suppose I *did* feel suffocated," Augustus admitted.

"But that didn't make you run?"

"I thought so too at first but intertwined with all of those feelings, I felt a need to come to this exact place. It needed me."

"The tree?" she asked as if unsure.

"The roots were rotting."

"You can speak to trees?"

"Not like how we're speaking, no, but the forest does whisper to adept ears. This forest is ill, Selina."

"This isn't a forest, it's a park."

"Precisely, I can feel the pain of its limitation. Seedlings trapped beneath the cement begging for sunlight. It's quite disturbing," he explained.

"That sounds agonizing. I can't begin to understand what it must be like for you in this city," she empathized.

"The balance between man and nature is destroyed."

"Perhaps that's true, but right now, we must go to my apartment and figure out our next steps."

"I am disinclined to return to that chaos. I think I am safest here," he said sturdily. Selina frowned. She understood his hesitation to leave.

Arguing with him may not be the best idea in his present state of emotion. She thought of a different way to approach the subject.

"You saw Kent with the gun before I did. Why did you save me?" Selina asked.

"You can't fool me with clever distractions."

"Please just answer," she pleaded. He looked away in protest.

"He meant to kill you," he stated flatly. "Or drag you back to En Tutum to torture you."

"But why did you intervene? Why did you risk yourself in such a weakened state?"

"I am beholden to you. You are Meh-Mon. It was my duty."

"Is it not your duty then, to protect me now?"

"Selina," his mind said to hers.

"You know more about this than I do," she answered out loud. "You got us out of Canada. *You* thought of the gold. We are here because of you."

"You freed me, ended a curse meant to last a thousand years or more. Who knows?"

"I did, didn't I?" She smiled. His eyes brightened at the sight of her happiness.

"Selina."

"Augustus… Will they stop looking for us? Do you think they could just let us leave without consequences?"

"It's more than that." He hesitated.

"What is it?"

"The truth is, I am afraid. You *freed* one of the nine, and I am sure you didn't know the implications. You just reacted to the cat's death. But it *won't* matter. The Aprīcōrum will show no mercy to either of us."

"The people who cursed you."

"Yes! Powerful progenies to the God of Light and guardians of humankind. They will not risk the curse to be weakened any further."

"I didn't free you on my own. I called upon many. If you weren't worthy, they wouldn't have helped me."

"Selina," he said again softly.

"When I met my mother, she warned me of the torment you'd experience if I didn't intervene. It was the mitigating factor that forced me to leave her side. You still feel bad for what they did, maybe even responsible, but don't you dare imply to me you were not worth saving."

"Perhaps you must hear more of the dreadful past," he said as if he loathed bringing up the past.

"Tell me whatever you need, at my apartment. This park gets dangerous at night."

"You need not fear any creature while I am by your side."

"It's not the creatures I'm worried about," she sighed.

CHAPTER 20

WE ARE
NOT SAFE HERE

"Place your palms on top of my palms," he instructed, sensually. "Now, focus on the path to your home."

"Just think about it?" she asked, losing patience. Night will arrive soon; she did not want to encounter the people trolling the park after dark.

"Yes. Close your eyes and visualize you and I leaving this willow. Where do we turn?"

"Okay."

"Imagine yourself light as a rose petal. You can go through anything."

A soft light shone through her eyelids; she squinted them open to take a peek. Remarkably, the park appeared as it did before but differed slightly. Their journey, the trees, the streets, the sky all tinted with a tangerine hue as if the world now existed under a veil of their combined magic. The concern plaguing her a moment ago vanished also. Selina's gnawing urge to exit the park was gone too.

"Show us the way," Augustus said from behind her. "Jump over the pond," he alluded. "It'll be fun."

Her legs obeyed without hesitation. She stepped out from under the willow tree and completed a flying leap over the pond to reach the road on the other side. She jumped unnaturally and unimaginably high, floating slowly, then landed securely on her own two feet. Beside her, Augustus excitedly took the leap too. The experience resembled a euphoric dream state. Was she flying? It certainly felt so. Perhaps drifting described it better or gliding on the October evening air. She wanted to ask how she was able to achieve this capability. Was this still her vision? She felt the words on her lips ready to come out, but she laughed instead.

"This *is* fun!" she exclaimed. Augustus nodded in agreement, beaming the happiest smile she'd ever seen on him. He looked like an entirely different person—free of worry, strikingly handsome, cheery gray eyes twinkling like diamonds—and it felt just as precious to witness. His jovial demeanor endowed her with great affection for him. Attraction, even. In this atmosphere of enchantment, he possessed a regal confidence he never displayed before. She watched his hair sway in slow motion, like a merman underwater. Conquered by his newfound allure, she looked away shyly.

The sidewalks were completely empty, a detail Selina did not notice. There weren't any cars on the streets, either. She jumped again, reaching as high as the traffic lights. They skipped, ran, somersaulted—all while giggling. She stopped abruptly and rather awkwardly in front of a high-rise condominium so tall, it made Augustus dizzy when he looked up, attempting to see the top of it.

"This is my building." Selina announced giddily.

"Have we reached your lodgings?"

"No way, this structure contains a lot of *lodgings*," she chuckled. "My apartment is upstairs." Hand in hand, both entered. Selina led them to the building's two elevators.

"Is there another way up?" Augustus asked.

"Yes, the stairwell, but it's pretty isolated. Creepy."

"That will be the choice, then."

They jumped, playfully skipping stairs as they went up seventeen flights.

"I don't feel the weight of myself." Selina observed happily.

"You are as light as a dandelion spore."

"You keep saying that" she laughed.

"It's important!" They exited the stairwell gleefully. She walked to her apartment door.

"Wait, I can't grab my keys. Why can't I touch the knob?"

"It's because you are not really here."

"Not really where? Here, in this hallway?"

"Take a deep breath and brace yourself."

"For what?"

"To become tangible again."

Two loud voices suddenly filled the otherwise quiet hallway. The conversation emanated from an apartment across the hall. The noise increased as if the occupants approached their door to the hallway.

"Oh shit. It's my neighbor Jenny," she panicked. "She cannot see us here," Selina said, still disoriented.

"She will not see us," he interjected in a knowing tone, still brandishing his striking smile. For reasons unknown, her worries crumbled away. She hadn't experienced this kind of freedom from her own mind since $2 tequila Tuesdays at her local college pub.

Both of them heard the clinking sounds of Jenny's door unlocking.

"They're definitely gonna see us," she giggled, "and then our cover will be blown to shit."

Augustus seized Selina's arm aggressively. She cried out startled, still laughing as if inebriated. Without haste or time to explain, he walked through the closed door and pulled Selina along with him inside the apartment, just as her neighbor stuck her head out.

"We walked through a locked door," she laughed. "What the Frock? Did you kill me? Are we ghosts?"

He grabbed her palms without asking. Augustus whispered Latin words. His eyes glowed an orange color, similar to the tangerine hue encompassing their current excursion.

"Your eyes are weird," she pointed out. Quickly, the color coming from his eyes surrounded his hands, which were holding hers. At that same moment, she became very aware of gravity and the weight of her own body. "I feel like I'm filling up with quicksand," she said, no longer smiling. She attempted to take a step away from Augustus and collapsed on her living room floor. "My legs don't work!" she exclaimed. "Please tell me what the hell just happened to us."

"Your atoms and molecules are rebinding; you're becoming whole again."

"I think I'm going to hurl." She retched. Jenny's voice outside of her apartment door induced silence from the couple.

Selina froze, afraid of making any indication of her presence known. Their only advantage was the element of surprise. She wanted everyone to assume she was foraging through the Canadian outdoors, maybe lost or possibly dead. *It's safer for everyone, most of all, Augustus.* The two stood completely still on the other side of Selina's door until they heard Jenny's door close.

"You say you're a forest dweller. I can understand you being able to detect sick trees. How do you know the other stuff? How did you turn us into ghosts? How did you know how to pull us through a closed door?" Selina asked seriously. "Are you a warlock?"

"A what?" he replied, perplexed.

"A warlock? A male witch? If you are, you have to tell me. It's the warlock's code." Augustus laughed at her insinuation. Selina's frustration grew.

"I am the descendant of humans and faeries. I draw my power from the spirits of the forest. You are impressed by parlor tricks, my maiden; your true power is far superior."

"My *true* power?" she repeated. "I'm still trying to wrap my head around all of this. I'm a sophomore at Barnard College. Before meeting you, my *true* power was acing exams after binge-watching a show all night."

"But you are also Meh-Mon."

"You keep saying that."

"The mark on your hand, that crescent shape, that is the mark of Meh-Mon."

"Seriously?" Selina asked, shocked.

"My sister's hand bore the same scar. You may be all the things you say. But you are also Meh-Mon."

"Edha noticed the mark," Selina admitted. "She saw it my first night there."

"Then we are in more of a situation," Augustus predicted. "She will undoubtedly inform the others. We are not safe here."

CHAPTER 21

EDHA'S RANGE

J ust as he said that: *Bang. Bang. Bang.* Someone pounded on her front door.

"Police, open up!" a tough-sounding man yelled from the hallway.

"If we ignore them, can they get inside?" Augustus asked calmly.

"Yes, with cause, they have the right to break it down!" More banging.

"We're trapped in here." Selina panicked, still sprawled on the floor. Augustus picked her up and held her close against his chest. He lifted his right arm high above his head while clutching her with his left.

"Velum," he murmured to himself. Out of the elevated hand, purple light exited. Quickly, it orbited around Selina and Augustus, beginning from the tops of their heads to their feet before disappearing.

"We are cloaked. As long as they do not touch us, they will not know we are here." Selina decided to hide in her walk-in bedroom closet. She determined it was the only place that could keep both of them safe from colliding with the officers.

"You do not have to break the door down," they heard Jenny protest outside of her door. "I have her key."

Four armed officers charged inside the open door, stomping heavily as they entered.

"She's not here," Jenny protested from the hall. "Is there a gas leak or something?" Her questions went unanswered. From the closet, they heard the officers searching each room.

"Clear!" a voice yelled from the bathroom.

Another officer yanked open the bedroom closet. A brawny middle-aged officer, sporting a blonde buzz cut, scanned the area for his suspect. Augustus's magic kept them unseen.

"All clear, boss," the obnoxious officer said unreasonably loud into his mobile phone. "The bed is still made, stove's cold, the garbage cans are all empty, plus the front desk guy said he hasn't seen her since she left on the trip."

"That's the boss?" a thinner, younger officer asked, entering the bedroom. "You tell 'em she ain't here?"

"No, numbnuts, I said we're arresting her right now," he answered sarcastically, after ending the call.

"Jeez, no need to get on my case. You've been riding me all day, Danny. What gives?"

"Sorry, Paul. I skipped my meal break for this shit. I hate it when they call last minute," Danny said, still irked.

"What did this girl do? All this hoopla, for what?" Paul asked, scratching his black hair with a pen. "I have a kid sister her age."

"I think she stole something from Canada. Their mayor called our mayor. It's very political. Way high above our pay grade," Danny stated informally.

"She lives in a place like this, and she steals?"

"California girls are crazy. No rhyme or reason for what they do."

"Isn't your wife from Cali?" Paul asked. They shared a laugh while exiting.

* * *

I think she stole something from Canada. The officer's words repeated in Selina's head. She had never stolen anything in her life. Brett and Kate raised her with integrity. She hardly ever told a lie. She remembered the last time she lied to Brett.

Selina was nine years old. She'd just lied about eating Kate's croissant. Brett picked her up and carried her into his work study.

"Some of the world's best stories are lies, made-up characters from a made-up place and time. Movies and music—art, actors and kings and queens; all lie. I lie. The world is so stupendously boring. Why not improve it with creation?" Brett said as Selina stared at her feet, guilt-ridden. She knew he *knew* the truth. Her heart broke.

"Children have the best imaginations of all. There's magic and wonder in your little heads. Everything is new. Everything is possible. There very well could be a princess somewhere off in the far deep part of the world. Maybe she is happy? Maybe she is curious? Maybe she must go on an adventure to discover hidden treasures?" Brett continued.

"You have to decide what kind of person you want to be right now. Do you want to improve the world or deceive it? You know what deception is?" he asked. Little Selina nodded. "You know what it means to tell a person something with the idea of robbing them from the truth?"

Tears accumulated and tickled the corners of her eyes. She nodded again, letting the tears trickle out and run down her cheeks. Brett knelt on one knee and wiped away her tears with his thumbs.

"Did you eat your mother's croissant?" he asked. Without looking at him, she nodded for the third time.

"Sweetie, we don't lie to the people we love. Telling lies hurts people's feelings, and you don't want to deceive your old dad, do you?" He lifted her head from facing the ground to face him.

"No, Dad," she cried. "I'm sorry." He hugged her tight as she continued to cry and kissed her on both cheeks afterward. Selina felt bad for days.

Twelve years ago, she vowed to embrace a virtuous life, however unpopular. It *felt* good to be good. As evident by the eaten croissant incident, she didn't handle guilt well.

To hear the officers accuse her of stealing hurt her immensely. Selina worried about the press finding out. The irony of the predicament annoyed her. As soon as she understood fame, she avoided doing anything to appear in the tabloids. Now, if this news spread, she'd be labeled a thief regardless of what was true. Aside from that rage. She was beginning to understand Edha's power and range. It would appear she may be aligned with politicians. The challenge to avoid her substantially increased.

CHAPTER 22

A FAERIE THING

T he door closed hard behind the trespassers. Nightfall crept on them. They stood in the closet a couple of minutes to be sure their visitors were truly gone. Augustus was the first to leave the closet. He said a few words, placing his palm on the front door. It glowed the same purple color of protection.

"These lodgings are safe," he proclaimed. "This door will not open again from the outside unless set on fire." Selina sat with her back toward the wall of the closet.

"Did you hear me?" he asked. "We are safe here for as long as we need to be."

Selina did hear him, but his words offered no comfort. She knew she would not be able to stay hidden in that apartment forever. Worrying would have to wait. Hunger struck them both very suddenly. Selina realized when they ate last, Augustus was still a cat! They hurried to the kitchen.

"I can cook us hot dogs," Selina suggested to Augustus as she rummaged through her fridge.

"Hot dogs? Is it a meal made of dog?" he reacted with disgust.

"No. A hot dog like a frankfurter; a sausage."

"Is it comprised of meat?"

"Yes."

"What kind?" he asked, but by his expression, she knew he was not interested.

"Okay. Forget hot dogs. I can make us some hamburgers. Surely, you've heard of those?" she wondered. "Maybe En Tutum served it?"

"And this is also comprised of meat?"

"Yes. Let me guess, you don't eat meat?"

"While a cat, of course. Before my curse, my people enjoyed fresh vegetables. Bread. Meatless stews. We did not hunt animals for sustenance. Or worse, raise them from infancy to slaughter them when adults. We found those practices barbaric."

"Humans are carnivores," she said quickly in response. She participated in this type of debate before, many times with the vegetarians she encountered. "Our bodies need meat to function."

"Exactly so. *Humans* are carnivores," he emphasized. "I am not *fully* human; therefore,

I can opt out of flesh consumption. The earth provides me with all I need to survive."

"You say 'earth,' and I think dirt; do you mean the planet Earth? I'm really trying to understand."

"Faeries are non-corporeal life forms. They can appear and take shapes, even partake in all functions like mating, for a time. Their true essence is pure energy. My genetics are unique, to say the least," he answered proudly. "When I say earth, I mean everything grown from soil. Fruit, wheat, nuts, rice."

"Wait. What we did earlier from the park to my apartment? When we were ghosts, for lack of a better saying? That was a faerie thing? We were non-corporeal floating and flying around town?"

"'A faerie thing' is an oversimplification, but yes. I can enter a parallel world, created by faeries to mirror this one exactly."

"Why didn't we just go there in the first place? Sounds to me like an ideal hiding spot."

"I assumed time was of the essence," he answered informatively. "The walk would've taken over thirty days. Besides, it cannot sustain life; its sole purpose is for safe passage and ..." He froze.

"And what?"

"Dark faeries sometimes trapped human children there as punishment to their parents."

"To kill them!"

"Not directly, but yes, luring children there did lead to their deaths," he said reluctantly.

"How?"

"Dehydration, I suppose? Hunger?"

"Both are long and painful. Shame on them."

"Actually, no. It's a happy place. No suffering allowed. I know you felt it, the short time you were there." And then she remembered she *did* feel happy, carefree, and drawn to Augustus.

"Even happy, it's still a messed-up way to go."

"Agreed."

"I can make you a sandwich made from nuts and grapes. Wanna try?"

"Yes. Please."

She proceeded to fix them both peanut butter and jelly sandwiches, which were deliciously enjoyed on her couch.

"Let me get these." She said gesturing for their sticky plates.

"Please let me." He insisted.

"Have you ever washed a dish?" Selina asked teasingly.

"No but I am a quick study." He countered. Augustus followed her in the kitchen carrying his won used plate.

While placing his dish in the sink, the sleeve on his shirt briefly flickered. For a split second, the entire shirt became translucent. Had Augustus been sitting as she asked, the slight anomaly might have gone unseen. Instead, she *did* see it. For the short time his skin was visible, she observed various discolorations, cuts, bruises, and dried blood!

"Your shirt, I saw through it," she declared. "You're hurt." Augustus glanced down at his clothing, wearing an expression of betrayal.

"Oh yes, it took quite a lot of energy to protect this place," he said elusively.

"But clothes are clothes. It's solid, fabric, tangible. Why could I see through it? And just how bad are the wounds I saw?"

"Clothes *are* clothes," he repeated. "Excellent assessment." Selina squinted her eyes at him suspiciously.

"What are you not saying?" she asked outright. "You're being weird." Augustus avoided eye contact. "Wait, are you still naked?"

"To the eyes, no. I casted a glamour of illusion."

"Oh my. This whole time, you've been actually naked? Walking with your bare feet?"

"It's not a big deal. I can't feel the elements," Augustus reminded her.

"Show me your true self."

"I'm embarrassed now. Please leave the matter be."

"I can't ignore what I saw. Augustus, un-glamour yourself."

"I am a gentleman. It's highly inappropriate."

"Can you heal yourself?" she asked with urgency. "Do faeries or half-faeries have the ability to recover from harm?" Augustus's shoulders slouched; he thought about lying if he thought she'd believed him.

"No," he said. "We cannot."

"Then this is a medical matter!" Selina argued. "It's not up for debate."

He slowly and reluctantly motioned his pointer finger toward himself. His attire, including the footwear, vanished in a puff of smoke. When the smoke dissipated, Selina gasped at the sight. The man instinctively covered his private area, yet Selina's eyes dared not disrespect him.

Each arm bore cuts, she assumed from branches and needle-sharp leaves. His legs exhibited the same slashes, some deeper than others. His entire body was crusty with dried blood stains and mud. He stood before her utterly humiliated, averting his eyes everywhere else.

Selina ran to her bathroom. Augustus heard her turn on a water source.

She returned, holding two beach-sized towels.

"Wrap this around you." She tossed him one of the massive towels. He grabbed it and did as was instructed. "I know you've probably never been in a shower before…" She paused. "But you have to get in. Those gashes need to be cleaned." He nodded in agreement.

He followed her into the bathroom, where he heard the water running.

"Check the temperature," she suggested. "See if it's too hot or too cold." He did as was told.

"It's fine."

"Drop the towel and step into the glass doors." Augustus bore an expression of further discomfort. He intentionally gazed up at the ceiling as he let the towel go.

"Oh, for crying out loud," she complained. She undid her boots quickly, stepping out of them.

"Wait, what's that noise? What are you d-doing?" Augustus stuttered. Selina unbuckled her belt, unfastened her jeans, and pulled them down.

"You didn't step in," she observed, while pulling off her sweater.

"I am aware of that fact. I am used to bathing a little differently, pardon," he answered in a worried tone. She touched the back of his shoulder; he nearly jumped out of his skin. "I realize this is not an act of voyeurism—for that, I am certain. You gain no pleasure in this. It's just demoralizing."

"It's fine. We're getting in together," Selina told him. "Please step in, so I can step in."

Eventually, Selina moved him aside and walked into the glass doors of her shower, still wearing her bra and panties. The water immediately undid her bun; her hair fell to her shoulders.

"Come now, it's only water." She smiled.

He stepped in.

"I'm not afraid," he said finally. "It's a show of respect."

"Women behaved differently wherever you come from, I understand." She reached to remove the showerhead off its base. "It's an adjustment for both of us, believe me." She pointed the warm flowing water to Augustus's chest. He flinched a bit at its force.

"Present day, this is how we bathe. Hold this." He took the showerhead from her and kept it pointing at him. Selina grabbed her body wash.

"Along with water, we use soap." She poured a generous amount of bodywash onto a washcloth. "The soap may cause your cuts to sting, but it's a good thing. It's rinsing the dirt away." She placed the washcloth on his chest. In circular motions, she dabbed his neck and shoulders. The scent of lavender filled the room as she lathered him.

The soap did sting his wounds, a LOT! Yet, he could barely focus on anything other than Selina's kind, concerned, beautiful face. He watched as her hair coiled up into bountiful S-shaped curls. The shower droplets thickened her eyelashes. It made him think of spider legs—spider lashes, he recalled the term. Her dark brown eyes possessed an amber tone in bright places, he observed.

From his point of view, Augustus could trace the water flow down past her perfect full lips, to her neck, and then…

Despite his gentlemanly nature, he couldn't help but notice Selina's ample, cantaloupe-sized bosom underneath her soaked bra. She gently turned him around. His back displayed various lacerations. Based on her examination, his top half didn't exhibit any wounds in need of stitches. She decided to allow him the dignity of surveying his bottom half.

"Okay, you get the gist." She stopped. "I'll let you wash your man parts in peace." She grazed past his naked body and exited the shower. "Please pay extra attention to the bottoms of your feet. Be careful; soap on your feet makes them slippery. Try not to fall."

CHAPTER 23

I WIN!

Augustus let the warm water cascade from the top of his head onto his face, neck, shoulders, back, etc. The droplets beating down on his scalp relaxed him. Mimicking Selina, he poured more of the lavender body wash on the cloth she'd handed him. He enjoyed the scented, soft suds on his skin. Lather. Wash. Rinse. He repeated the process at least four times.

He relished covering his entire body with soap. It also pleased him to stand directly under the showerhead and feel the water pull the substance off his skin. He dared to admit his contentment. He greatly enjoyed his first bathing since he'd been turned back.

He emerged from the bathroom forty minutes later, ghostly pale and shriveled.

"My, someone looks a full shade whiter," Selina joked. "How was it?"

"A bit confining at first," he confessed, "but that's been my experience since I boarded the aircraft."

"Even right now, in this apartment?" she asked. "As New York City apartments go, this is huge!"

"Before my curse, I preferred sleeping under starlight." His smile grew excitedly. "Jackson and I ..." He stopped. The mention of his sister's husband reminded him of his promise. A gloom surfaced on his face, right where the smile had been.

"What?" she edged. "Oh, c'mon." Yet his transformation from happy to a heavy-hearted, sorrowful expression made her let the topic be. She knew he suffered silently. She didn't want to force him to share feelings he'd rather keep to himself. She decided to walk out of the living room to give him a few minutes.

"No more magical clothes for you." She reentered the area carrying various garments in both arms. "I bought these for BJ, my brother, Brett Junior, for when he came to visit. There are pajamas, T-shirts, sweatpants, socks, slippers, all never worn. They might fit you a little loose. Luckily, the slippers do not need to fit perfectly."

"Which articles am I to bedeck myself in?" he queried. "There are too many selections to choose from."

"Okay. I guess you can wear pajamas for now." She chose the knitted Ralph Lauren sleepwear set. It included a soft gray long-sleeve fitted shirt along with red plaid pajama bottoms. "I'm gonna grab a shower myself. You'll be okay in the meantime?"

Selina hurried into the restroom, quickly closing the door behind herself. In that exact moment, she suddenly realized just how badly she needed a breather. A few moments alone without cohesive thoughts. Her arm reached for the hot water nozzle, more out of habit than command. Before long, steam filled the entire room as it had many times before.

The college student liked the water as hot as she could stand it, without causing burns. As she stepped into the glass doors of her shower, she vowed not to think about her current predicament. *Are we fugitives? At what lengths will the hunters go to apprehend us? And then what? Execution? Will Augustus be killed for my act of liberation?*

The steamy water came in contact with her toes first. The intense temperature of the shower effectuated a sedative-like temperament; a soothing, calming barrier formed, where stress and worry could not penetrate.

Augustus remained in the same spot on the couch. However, his modern-day clothing and freshly showered hair gave him the look of a model. His blue-black tresses, usually on his shoulders, adopted a curly disarray, messy as if fashionably on purpose appearance.

The pajamas originally intended for a brawnier defensive tackle football-playing teenager loosely fit its current wearer. Selina could've easily placed him in a high-end billboard or magazine ad for Ralph Lauren.

Certainly, she noticed his attractiveness before. It occurred as a glimpse here and there while they ran for their lives, escaping one danger after the other. Perhaps, in this instance, she saw it clearly because no immediate threat existed. They were just two people tucked away in a magically protected dwelling: safe.

Selina's return stole his attention. Her hair remained an abundance of soft, shiny curls. The red wine-colored satin nightgown she wore provided a voluptuous silhouette of her shape. *Regality becomes her,* he thought. Along with strength and courage, he'd be blind not to notice her exquisite looks.

"You're smiling," he mentioned. "I don't suppose you'd want to share your thoughts?" She waved away his words, a bit caught off guard. No way she wanted him to know how she fawned over him, however brief.

"I had a really good shower," she omitted. "I feel so relaxed now. How about you? Are you in pain? Did any of those abrasions need further attention?" He squinted his eyes suspiciously at her. She wondered if he detected her desperation to change the subject. *Get it together*, she urged herself. *He's not even all the way human!*

"The astute care I received remedied my discomforts," he stated with sincerity. "I'm truly indebted to you." He looked away bashfully. "The list of reasons to thank you grows longer."

"I probably owe you the same amount of thanks, if not more. You *did* get stabbed in the heart for me," she replied as a matter of fact.

"Right!" Augustus testified excitedly. "I win." Selına laughed. He displayed every emotion outward. The people she knew, herself included, hid their feelings by default. In her society, oversharing emotions meant weakness. The ability to keep one's composure through every encounter was seen as a strength. As she watched his glacier-gray eyes shimmer with contentment, she could not help but return his happiness. Knowing the horrors tomorrow faced, why not smile today?

She sat on the couch, leaving the middle cushion between them.

"Are you sleepy yet?"

"A little…"

"Now is the time to tell you more about the nine. I must tell you the story of Masayori, the worst of us. You will understand the weight of freeing one of the nine and why we are hunted viciously."

* * *

The Shogun, the most powerful officer in Japan second only to the emperor, who some believed was only superior in politics.

"Shogun Haruto Kamakura married a kind woman, who bore him twin sons. Unfortunately, the boys were not two when their mom succumbed to an unknown sickness. And the entire Kamakura clan grieved for a time. The widow's cousin Kiku elected to care for the boys until the shogun chose another bride. Yet, one year almost to the day, both boys mysteriously fell ill. Fearing a spreading pandemic, Kiku burned the boys' bodies when they died. Regrettably, their father was away to war at the time. Months later, Kamakura returned to discover his only children dead and burned. In addition, the few nights he reluctantly spent with Kiku resulted in a surprise pregnancy, with a new set of twin boys. He waited until the boys reached five years of age before marrying their mother. Kiku bore two more sons and a daughter. A full decade passed before Kamakura could finally love his children with Kiku. He feared illness, death, misfortune, and as his list of enemies grew, he feared retaliation. The children led healthy full-privileged lives, and no harm came to them until…."

"Until what?" Selina yawned, fighting to stay awake.

"On Masayori's eighteenth year of life, he kneeled on what would be the deathbed of his caretaker, Lee, a former monk who left the monastery to surreptitiously care for a toddler he found nearly drowned sixteen years prior.

"Lee confessed to Masayori that he was a Kamakura, rightful heir to the shogun's legacy. The monk was one of a few people who remembered the shogun's first wife and couldn't deny the resemblance any longer. She visited his monastery many times.

"But more than that, Masayori's survival meant the death of his brother was not the result of an illness. Someone *meant* to murder them. Someone thought they had murdered them both. With great detail, Lee shared the boy's history, stories of his mother, father, and departed twin brother. He also explained the shogun's difficulty to love his new children.

"Masayori returned to the Kamakura estate during a time when the shogun was away at war. He confronted Kiku, who admitted being responsible for the death of his brother and mother. She plunged a knife into his chest, narrowly missing his vital organs. But some say the black dagger did pierce his heart, turning it black against all mankind forever. Once again, he felt his body tossed into the river as he clung to life. That day, he felt the presence of his mother and twin brother. Masayori believed the spirits of his fallen family pulled him out of the water.

"Lee, the closest person he had to a parent, taught him peace, serenity, humility. If Masayori never discovered the truth about his birthright, there very well may never be a story to tell. But the rage in him knew no bounds, and whatever peace he learned got lost in the grief and suffrage of his history. When he recovered his chest wound, his first instincts were to return to the Kamakura estate to annihilate everything drawing breath under that roof."

Through his peripheral vision, Augustus saw a sleeping Selina, her arm nestled under her head on the far-right end of the couch. He smiled.

"Selina," he said softly, "let's bring you to bed." She walked clumsily to her bedroom with him as her escort. He waited until after she lied down.

"Lay with me," she said, half awake. "Right beside me." She patted the unoccupied portion of the bed. He walked around slowly and sat down.

"Under the covers," she directed. He lifted himself, allowing her to pull the covers down.

Once situated, she nuzzled up to him, placing her head on his chest. He cradled her awkwardly. He was very aware of her soft skin, despite the satin nightgown. The fabric was so thin he felt her curves through it. She smelled good. And he couldn't deny how splendidly he enjoyed her touch.

He had never been in a bed this soft. He doubted if he ever lied on a mattress. The foam material contoured to his muscles nicely. If this wasn't perfect contentment, he didn't know what was. He lied awake, listening to the sounds of her sleeping until darkness finally embraced his mind with rest.

Wake up
Wake up
My sister is knocking at the door!

Selina whacked his leg again. Augustus shot up from bed. She had already been awake long enough to change clothes. She wore jeans and a white thermal shirt. He also noticed her hair back in the curly bun.

"It's Haley!" she said, horrified. "What do I do?"

CHAPTER 24

THE STONE
OF AFFLICTION

"If there is even a 1% chance that that's really Haley, I can't risk my neighbor seeing her, or anyone else questioning her, snatching her up even, holding her hostage, or hurting a fucking hair on her head. She's my little sister.

"I would affirm the same proclamation of Abigail, but you must calculate the likelihood that it is an illusion. You cannot deny the situation's happenstance, despite your callowness. You are newly gifted; you are not responsible for the things you have yet to learn. But you *have* experienced glamour! You saw the clothes on my body, the shoes on my feet; you touched the cloth and heard the leather clatter against the concrete.

You may very well have seen boot prints in the soil; it is how illusion operates. It shows you what you expect to see, what you want to see," he uttered frantically in need of her favor. But even as he spoke, he already saw the decision in her eyes to open the door. He watched her pupils lead away from him, his voice, his eyes, his advice. In painstakingly slow motion, he saw her wrist rise to reach for the door. He knew what he knew. He hoped his heart was prepared for what came next.

Augustus's eyes widened with apprehension as he watched Selina twist the knob to her apartment. He braced himself, knowing her doing so broke his protective magic seal and left them open to attack. In a purple flash over the corners of the door, the magic shield ceased to exist.

She opened the door slowly. Immediately she noticed several boots on the ground along with the familiar quilted dressing gown under a bright red parka. Realizing her heart-wrenching mistake, she tried slamming the door shut, but it was too late. The door flung open at top velocity, at which she turned to Augustus utterly terrified.

"Crepidine," Edha chanted, waving a red-hot stone at Augustus. He let out a cry so daunting it made Selina's soul shiver. She turned in his direction, aghast at the discovery. He dropped to his knees, screaming in pain. Blood leaked through the man's fingers as he covered his face with his hand. "An eye for an eye, feline," Edha sneered finally. "Mr. Woodrow sends his regards from the hospital, a place where your paws put him!" The sight of his suffering inspired a cyclone of rage throughout Selina. This was, in fact, all *her* fault. Had she listened to him— had she trusted him to know better—then they'd be safe. *Foolish idiot,* she thought to herself. She raised her hands in defense of him. Fury awoke the magic inside of her, evident by her glowing yellow irises. Yet before Selina invoked the power growing within her, Edha's guards shot her with a stun gun. Two barbed darts burrowed into her abdomen. Jolts of electricity excruciatingly coursed through her. She hit the ground hard in a large thud, shaking in paralyzing agony.

"Do you think him to be a benevolent one? An innocent, peaceful kitty cat you can keep for your very own?" Edha asked rhetorically as Augustus writhed in pain. "He's a murderer, tried and convicted of the most contemptible acts against mankind. He and his party of filth set in motion a violence this world has never seen. The nine are responsible for the hundreds of thousands of souls dragged out into the streets and set on fire, for having so much as a twinkle of magic in their eyes. Women like my great-grandmother Faja, sentenced to die alongside her lineage of female descendants, stoned, brutalized, burned alive. No trial, no judge, just an ever-spreading terror of those daring never to risk another nine. I bore witness to the ruthlessness unleashed because of them. My adolescent eyes watched human skin blister, bubble, and eventually melt off the bone of some person who may not have ever yielded any magic at all." Selina stirred but failed to muster the strength to rouse herself.

"What do you suppose the Aprīcōrum will do to a girl so powerful as she, one whose magic can undo a curse that took ten elders to execute?"

"Leave her," Augustus commanded barely above a speaking tone. Blood and green puss oozed down his cheeks as he tried desperately to manage the incapacitating agony he underwent. All he could do was clutch the wounded eye, which bubbled in its socket.

"The puppeteer protects the puppet," Edha laughed. "How terribly uninteresting. I wonder whose strings you'll pull once she's dead?" The older woman's words infected Augustus with trepidation. These people meant to end them both. If successful, his sacrifice as a cat, her breaking his curse, their efforts in between to survive, all rendered meaningless.

"*Selina,*" his mind said to hers. No reply, just the feeling of her suffering.

"Tie her up tightly in that chair," Edha ordered the guard still holding the stun gun. "We need those devilish hands restrained and behind her back."

"What about him?" the other guard asked, referring to Augustus.

"This stone restores the balance of afflictions," she replied. "If I cut off your foot, it would remove mine to make our losses even in the duel, regardless of reasons, rights, or wrongs." The emerald stone lied dormant, dull in her hand; unlike a few moments prior, when it glowed red.

"Do we tie him up?"

"Here I am trying to teach you meatheads a thing or two about the dark arts, and you clatter on about nonsense. No. He will die of his wounds soon enough without medical intervention. No need to dirty yourself with him. I want him to suffer the same pain he caused."

"Apologies, Sheikha." The guard bowed as if in the presence of a royal. Edha nodded to dismiss them. All of her henchmen exited the living room to stand guard outside of the apartment.

"Wake up." She kicked the slippers on Selina's feet. "Let me tell you of a desperate time in history. More than two centuries before your birth. Amidst the campaign to abolish magic on this planet, a plan was devised. Imagine a crazy mob banged on your door, bearing torchlights and torture instruments. People of whom you see every day, even your own kin, demanding your execution. And how could you defend yourself? For many, their gifts are inherited. Ancestral magic is the most common type, like yours, I suppose. So why should you be punished for something you didn't choose to possess?" Edha reached into a small satchel and pulled out a glass orb.

"In ancient times, a few thousand years before the nine, tribes performed unspeakable rituals to keep the magic flowing in their village—blood sacrifices, even murders. But nothing comes without consequence. The gifts obtained from blood magic often caused madness to the receiver. After losing many young maidens, the elders devised a salubrious approach. A way to conserve the mind and still keep the force. A most powerful thaumaturge invented this spherical contraption. It can house magic and act as a catalyst to transfer power out of the charmed and into anyone else.

"Centuries later, to save their own lives, witches transmitted their magic into similar glass balls. It was done in hopes of resuming a normal life safe from the Aprīcōrum and the insane torch-carrying murderers who hated magic. And in time, when the hunters moved on, when they needed to tap into their power, they would dig the orb out of wherever it was deeply buried to get their magic back.

"Now, I believe you are free of wicked intentions. My people tell me you're a gifted college student. One with an extraordinary future laid upon her steps. Prevalent family ties. A strong emotional bond. Those people truly love you. You simply got swept up in Augustus's need to escape. He used you. He brought you into the forest and made you believe whatever he had to get free. I don't believe you should die for this mistake. Even I, once or twice in life, fell fool to a flickering silver tongue."

"What do you need me to do?" Selina groaned. "You obviously want something."

"He *will* die, deservingly so. Nothing you can do about it." She said plainly put, "You have to decide your own fate. You can come with me and allow me to collect your magic in this orb. After which, you're free to go on about your life. Finish your college degree. Meet a guy, marry, and have babies. *Live* the American dream."

"And if I refuse?" Selina asked. Edha frowned at the thought.

"Well, we certainly cannot have a person with your kind of gifts just walking around undoing curses that should never have been meddled with."

"So, if I give you all my magic, I live, and if I don't, I die?"

"I'm asking for your cooperation in filling this orb. The pleasant route. Although it can and will be filled without your consent. I'm in possession of some rather unpleasant totems of the compelling variety. You will do what I want either way."

"Totems?" Selina asked, mainly to stall.

"Witches on the run made magical objects to sell for profit. Once targeted, the Aprīcōrum never stopped hunting their subject. The pursued needed to eat, sleep, and run all on a moment's notice. That required money. So, in the dark, in silence, and in secret, they created these *dark objects* and sold them for a high price. Maybe someone wanted revenge. Maybe a broken heart sought requited love. Much like this stone I just used on Augustus: the stone of affliction.

"I've never been able to wield a magic wand myself, but I've always had the money to buy the most powerful tools on the market. You *will* put your magic in this orb; whether you survive it is up to you. Augustus shredded the eye of Mr. Woodrow. You remember the outdoorsman that foraged the woods at night to find you and save your life? He hangs on by a thread fighting bacteria brought on by cuts to his eye." Her cellphone rang. The ring looked as if it startled her, like she forgot she toted it on her person. She answered.

"WHAT!?" she yelled into the phone. "His heart gave out?" She brought the phone away from her face. "You think about it while I take this call. Have a decision ready!" She departed Selina's living room to speak more privately in the bedroom. They both heard the door close loudly.

CHAPTER 25

GIVE ME YOUR PAIN

E dha left Selina to think. Nothing would be easier than to go back to her life on schedule. She could resume her classes at Barnard College, go back to California, hang out with Brett, perhaps have another adventure. If she agreed, she could go back to her family, laugh with her sister Haley, maybe get fixed up on a couple of blind dates, see a movie, and drink a really good martini with her mom Kate. And maybe that would be enough. But would she ever truly forgive herself for not doing everything in her power to save the man who died for her? Could she ever go back knowing what she really inherited from her biological family? Even if she did her damnedest to pretend, to fake happiness to survive, she doubted it would be a life worth living without him.

"Do it," Augustus said to her mind secretly so Edha could not hear. *"It's okay, Selina."*

"Are you crazy?" she replied mentally. *"Just abandon you to die?"*

"*Yes*," he said flatly.

"But you'll DIE!" she screamed to him mentally.

"I am no longer cursed, thanks to you. Whatever lies ahead on the other side, my family will be there. I'm ready for it."

"Do you have a death wish? Why are you constantly volunteering to off yourself? It is not noble; it's inconsiderate."

"The pain. It's…it's crippling." He sighed. *"I can barely maintain this connection."* His voice tapered off a little. *"Do not let a swollen ego prevent you from concluding the easiest option."*

"Show yourself to me! Up here in my mind like you did before in the meadow. Let me see you."

"I'm weakened. And I fear…" Just the act of speaking seemed to tire him. *"I fear I lack the strength to grant such a grand request. I worry. My time has soon come."*

"What does that mean?" she asked, half fearing the answer. He did not clarify. Augustus's silence took the breath out of her body. *"Fine. If this is goodbye, if you want me to let you go forever, you have to come to me. Please, I must see you."*

"*I can't,*" he whispered

"*Draw from me,*" she begged, and then the idea rocketed in. *That's it!*

"*Selina.*"

"*Draw from me. You can do it. I'm right here.*"

He appeared similar to the way he first entered her life, slick with suffering, despair, and a corpse-like defeat. Unlike the willow tree in the meadow, Augustus brought them to a nondescript dark room. It lacked any specifics or details. She noticed him.

"You can barely stand," she said as an observation. Augustus tried to smile, but even his mental representation reflected the horror Edha inflicted. He abruptly fell to his knees.

"Your power is great," he said, "but I grow weaker by the second. I might not be able to give a fitting farewell." She knelt beside him, trying to figure out a way to execute the plan she'd already decided to act on.

"Hold out your arms."

"Selina."

"Do it!" she barked. *No time for politeness,* she thought, frenzied. With an intense effort, he managed to bring his arms out palms upward. She clasped his wrists aggressively. It startled him.

"What are you doing?" he groaned.

"Give me your pain!"

"My *what*?"

"Give me your pain. Give me the infection. Pour those woes into *me*. *Quickly!*"

"Now who's crazy?" he said dismissively, nearly succumbing to the fatigue threatening him.

"You call me all-powerful. *You* convinced me I'm this Meh-Mon type. My mother—my *real* mother, Elodie—told me I am the nexus. If I'm a fraction of what she thinks I am, I can handle it."

"I refuse to bequeath you with this torment. I won't risk your survival."

"But you're dying. And I'm strong," she asserted, only half believing it.

"The infection will kill you. No."

"I was born in the 21st century. I've been immunized. I survived the chickenpox, poison oak, the flu several times. I take my vitamins with my coffee. Trust me."

"I can't barter my life against yours."

"It's not bartering if you believe in me," she said with frustration. He looked away, uncertain.

"Enough." She stared down at his wrists. She attempted to imagine the illness flowing into his bloodstream.

"Selina, no."

"I don't know any fancy Latin words. I can't summon up my powers instantly with a word or wave, but I don't need any of those tricks," she said, more to herself than to him. She dropped his wrists hard onto his lap.

"I know who I am. I never felt more powerful than I do right now. You are asking me to let you die while I sit and watch. You're asking me to allow this woman to commit murder right before my eyes and go unchallenged." She felt heat rising from her groin into her stomach. "I don't know what the future holds, and I can't guarantee that I'll survive, but I'm prepared to fight like hell to preserve both our lives." She grabbed his wrists again, hard. He winced; her palm burned his skin.

With her eyes squeezed tight, she commanded her power to ease his pain; to seek out his ailments, discomforts, toxins. She demanded it to enter her. Forcefully, Selina's nails dug into his skin, causing him to bleed. Instantaneously, she saw the same nail prints on her. Augustus watched in astonishment while her magic circled his blood droplets emerging from the wounds she caused. His body stiffened. Soon after, he noticed a cooling sensation in the veins of the arm she impaired. He quickly discovered twinges of relief. His levels of suffering dipped from a screeching 100 to 96, then 94, and so on.

It's working. She said it's…

And that's when it hit her, like someone dropped acid on her pupil. She stumbled back, unable to control her faculties.

"Selina!!!" he yelled. She ended their mental link with one exhausting wave. He needn't see her trembling in anguish. She dared not allow him the ability to witness her regret. Her infected eye quickly spread around the entire orbital cavity.

Mr. Barton, her 8th-grade biology teacher, compared the body's immune system to an army. Any sign of intruders (which meant infection) and those white blood cells would swarm the enemy, attack it from all sides, and rip it apart. Behind his back, they used to call him farting-Barton. It's funny what the mind recalls when under extreme duress.

Fully present, back in the chair with her hands bound behind her back, she endured the consequences of her actions. The eye fizzed and festered in her socket, causing both sharp and dull throbs through the skull.

Imagine the army men, she thought to herself, frantic. Imagine endorphins, released and swimming ferociously to the brain.

Meditation! Think of the yellow willow tree under the orange pregnant moon. Remember lavender spores fluttering in the cool night air. Someone loves you here. She began formulating the scene in her mind. Doing so distracted her away from insufferable hurt.

CHAPTER 26

AFFLICTION UNDONE

The pomposity of her, he exclaimed to himself. Although Selina succeeded in relieving his physical discomforts, worry still managed to plague him. He drowned in perturbation. He despaired over her state of being. She severed their connection just as she took hold of his condition. He parted the fingers covering his eyes; dismayed, he learned his sight was almost nonexistent from the infected eye. Yet also grateful for Selina's gall to intervene when she did. Brain damage would've likely been the next, less survivable result of Edha's stone. As a precaution, he planned to veil himself with protection from dark objects. Selina too. He listened carefully. He heard Edha speaking on the phone.

The woman's loquacious tendency is a gift for once, he said to himself, thinking of the thousand occurrences in which he hated her long-winded (often one-sided) monologues. Yet this time, he would maximize the time he'd been given. *Talk your head off!*

With his remaining good eye, he glanced over at Selina. He shuddered at the sight of her slumped in the chair, appearing unconscious, as the infection bled down her cheeks. Even in this state, her strength and beauty gleamed.

He undid the ropes binding her wrists, all but 10%. He wanted them to still look tied up.

* * *

Edha walked back in with her phone conversation still on her mind. Kent Woodrow just experienced a cardiac event in the hospital. His aorta shredded. They were prepping him for the cardiothoracic surgeon to operate.

From behind, Selina appeared to have been sleeping. *How disrespectful!* Edha thought angrily. *She is supposed to be grappling with the decision of her life, and she's asleep.* She hurried her steps.

Augustus heard the bedroom door open. He ran to the floor in the same spot where he'd been lying, waiting to die. He lied down once more, and this time he vowed to fight for both of their lives. He sprawled himself out, fake-moaning in pain and rolling around, making sure he didn't stray too far away from the state she left him in. The tables *did* turn; he felt almost giddy with anticipation. There was nothing she could do to hurt them any longer. He completed the spell that protected against dark magic.

Edha walked to the front of Selina. She gasped in bewilderment at the sight of the girl's bleeding. She distinctly remembered the specifics of both of their injuries. Another glance affirmed Edha's suspicion further. She regarded the captee's sweating and trembling to mean something changed in her absence

"What the hell is going on?" she demanded aloud. Edha turned to search in her duffel bag a few steps away, perhaps to search for another totem. Forearms deep into the bag, Augustus decided to take advantage of yet another one of her distractions. He crept up on her. She turned around suddenly, holding what appeared to be a tarry pinecone in her hand.

"Back up," she commanded. "This will surely kill you, despite your annoying resilience. This will kill both of you!"

"Hand over the stone," Augustus said.

"No."

"You may think you know magic," he said, "but those totems are no match for me and definitely not her."

"You're a fool if you think you can incite fear in me. I know what you are. You're useless without the other eight. You won't scare me into doing anything, feline."

"Okay, but I can compel you to hand over the stone. Think. Before you find yourself doing something less approving."

"I will not," Edha declared with fearless eyes.

He pulled from behind his back a small wooden totem, identical to those paddleball, bounce-back games, without the ball and string. The outward-facing side of the totem, visible to Edha, illustrated special circular carvings— hypnosis lines or vortex swirls meant to spellbind the onlooker.

"I believe it was you, the charlatan who mentioned, nearly bragging, about the amount of compulsion totems you brought here," Augustus said, slightly smiling. "Give me the stone you used to harm me, now."

"No," Edha refused daringly. "Only an amateur would bring totems and not douse themselves in protection. Surely, you noticed by now that those don't work on me; none will." Augustus laughed.

"You need to know that we are also protected, so your bag of tricks is null and void."

"It appears we've reached an impasse," she concluded.

"Hardly," Augustus argued. "I can just murder you with my bare hands or compel your guards out there to do it, slowly."

"Murder me?" the woman asked as if genuinely surprised at his courage. "The weakest of the nine?"

"It isn't wise to antagonize me while my mercy thins."

"Go ahead, do your worst." Edha stood firm. In her cold eyes and hardened face, he realized she would call his bluff. Did he hate her enough to bludgeon her to death? Probably. Did he think she could die by his hands, less than likely? Edha's been alive for as long as he'd been cursed; two centuries at least. He wondered what evil delivered an unnaturally long life to her, and at what price? To save Selina, he'd likely go to great lengths. In order to do that, he needed the stone. Augustus decided to take another approach.

"His heart is collapsing, isn't it?" Augustus asked, and the potency of hatred in Edha's eyes softened briefly.

"What do you know of this?" she edged, trying to appear nonchalant.

"You meant to kill me with that stone. You failed. But now that I have survived your attack, the stone returns his afflictions back onto him," Augustus disclosed. "I might've blinded him as a cat, but he plunged a spear into my heart. He *killed* me." Edha looked away, dismayed. "If the stone of affliction evens the duel, it will mean his death."

"You lived," she said, barely audible.

"Magic intervened as it must now, or is your disgust for me so unwavering, you'd ignore the death of an innocent?"

"Don't presume to care for anything other than your own agenda."

"What say you!" Augustus commanded with force.

She pulled the stone out of a deep chest pocket located in her coat. Reluctantly, Edha tossed the stone before his feet.

"Incendia," he said without taking his eyes off his adversary. Together they watched the stone go up in flames, burning away any and all afflictions attached to it. As the last of the orange sparks diminished, he veered at Edha. Something resembling a warm expression displayed on her face. He could almost see traces of beauty hidden behind years of indifference. He wondered how long she played this game; two centuries, three? And to what end?

Selina rose up, quickly and coherently sound, completely recovered from the infection. When Augustus noticed how quickly her wounds healed, he blinked both his eyes in hopes of restoring the vision he lost when he grappled with the same disease. Yet deep down, he'd already accepted his damage as permanent. From Selina's point of view, Augustus and Edha stood opposite one another, clutching strange objects at the other. She wanted to kick him for not believing in her. Then again, considering she probably shouldn't have opened the door in the first place, maybe their scores were settled.

"What can I do?" Selina asked.

"Pick up two more compulsion totems," he said. "Her shield will likely shatter against the force of our powers combined, charmed or not." Edha rolled her eyes at the two of them. As much as she hated to admit defeat, she could not deny the victor in this circumstance. She tossed her bag at Selina, giving her access to the other compulsion totems.

Augustus and Selina stood side by side, both endowed with two compulsion totems, one in each hand. All four arms stretched outward in the direction of Edha.

"When you arrive home, you will feel accomplished and happy to have made the extra steps to ease your worries," Selina said, compelling Edha. "And you will be relieved. You can tell everyone that you've recovered any missing items stolen. This was all just a misunderstanding. Selina is not a thief."

"You came here to discover me and my boyfriend making out on the couch," she continued. "I am not a magical being. I'm just a normal, spoiled twenty-year-old in love. It turned out that same boyfriend surprised me in the woods that night, and we decided to fly back to the States on his family's private jet. You spoke to our parents, who happily cleared up any lingering concerns you had. The cat is dead. Kent murdered him, mistaking him for a lynx. You will not give any of this more than a moment's attention at a time. Go and never come back."

"I go," Edha repeated, appearing bewitched by the two totems each of them possessed.

"Return to En Tutum," Augustus instructed. "Tell everyone the cat is dead and the curse is still intact."

"There isn't magic left aside from your collection of dark totems. You've achieved your goal. This task is over. Go home and move on," Selina concluded.

"Go home," Edha echoed, dizzily.

Once compelling the guards outside, the two felt it best if they saw her all the way off. Both of them led Edha out of the building, into the company jeep, and eventually, onto the tarmac, where an En Tutum labeled G550 aircraft awaited her. After the woman climbed up the golden airstairs, right before the pilot led her inside, she stopped and turned back to the two escorts anticipating her departure. She smiled cunningly, enough to chill their spinal cords into icicles of frozen dread. Although brief, it cascaded the gloomiest shadow on their entire triumph. Suddenly, they pondered if it had been Edha's victory all along.

Maybe Edha faked the compulsion in order to leave an outmatched situation safely. There was no way to know for sure. Doubt shrouded over their feelings of success heavily. Neither one of them spoke a word during the ride back to the apartment.

CHAPTER 27

I CHOOSE YOU

B ack at the apartment, Selina offered him more clothing. His current attire exhibited heavy blood stains from his wound.

Augustus chose a sweatsuit, which also hung on his shoulders loosely. Luckily, the drawstring on the pants kept them from falling down. After he cleaned up, Selina assessed his injury. The sclera (usually white) part of the eye bore a fuchsia pink color. His cloudy, mucus-covered pupil caused alarming concern for his companion.

"Is the sight totally gone?" Selina frowned. Augustus nodded. "How are you not more upset by this?" she asked, still clutching his chin gently. Augustus stared into Selina's upturned chestnut-colored eyes. Her entire face furrowed with worry and concern.

"My injuries were assuaged, and my demise delayed, yet again because of you."

"If only I acted sooner," she sighed.

"And if you never acted?" he proposed. "What then?" Augustus brought her hands to his chest. "Your valor is unmet." Selina blushed, impressed by his choice of words.

"I expected you to heal, promptly, after the stone was destroyed."

"I hoped for that outcome as well. I suppose the infection already did its worst while in me. I am half-human; I do not bode well with infections. All the more reason to be grateful you intervened."

"Well, I probably shouldn't have opened the door in the first place." Augustus's good eye opened widely as if shocked. "Yeah, I said it," she admitted. "I own it." She sat beside him on her couch, still holding his hands. "I'm sorry to have done that to you."

"'Twas not you who held up the stone, against me. My dear."

"It might as well have been," Selina mumbled, guilt-ridden.

"I must tell you something before we are again in danger."

"Okay."

"As I watched the green leaves shrivel brown and fall, I longed for you. When the sunlight seared upon the glistening snow, blinding me, with eyes squeezed tight, I waited for you. As countless people walked by about their lives, rejecting me, perhaps not even seeing me at all, with a devastating ache of loneliness, I *endured* for you." He turned to face her.

"I believe I loved you into existence. My soul begged the universe for your creation. I knew you would save me. Rescue me from the deepest pits of sorrow where my heart has sunken. And so, you have. Easily. From the moment I met you and every moment, right up to this one, you are the quintessence of my happiness. Trust when I say, it's okay. I harbor no animosity over my injury. Meh-Mon, you cured more than you harmed."

Selina searched his eyes for embellishment but only found sincerity. His intensity frightened her a bit, and she gasped aloud when it hit her.

Brett and Kate loved her. She did have a family, a great family! Yet still, tears were dancing on the rims of her eyes. Augustus searched her face, puzzled. She herself felt puzzled. He gripped her hand as her tears fell.

She hadn't realized she also walked with the ache of loneliness. Everything about their encounter remained unreal. He brought a fresh batch of adventure into her life. He represented excitement, magic, and mystery. Yet her heart swelled, implying he meant more. A friend? She didn't want to know the answer.

"You're crying?" He tilted his head as if to question why. "My feelings are unrequited?" He looked away, dropping her hand into her lap. "You needn't answer," he nipped.

A loud buzz interrupted her thoughts. It was coming from the pocket she'd been sitting on. She compelled one of Edha's goons to iMessage her every hour with a progress report. Her screen read *5X5,* meaning they were still on course to their intended destination, and there were no unscheduled landings. When she looked back in his direction, he seemed upset.

"I lived my life as a triangle in a world of circles," she said to him softly. "Brett and Kate chose me. They took me out of that orphanage in Dominica. They loved me each and every day. I felt their love and protection, so it is not with malice to state that despite them, I remained a triangle."

"Do you feel as though they loved you, but not as their own?"

"Absolutely not. Their love could fill two oceans and still have enough left to fill a sea, for me. Both of them encouraged my uniqueness, supported *everything* me, but I couldn't exist in that bubble alone. It was outside of those doors and out in the world where I was shunned."

"Growing up, the girls at my school cared about photo shoots, videos, having the perfect hair and a favorable angle. Everything meaningful to them—designer labels from Beverly Hills, having followers, being famous—is all pointless to me. And of course, I'm the outcast weirdo that doesn't want to be in a thousand photos. I'd rather stop to smell a flower than snap a selfie. I even tried to bond over hiking, but I like hiking for the hiking, not for the pictures and hashtags." She noticed Augustus's struggle to understand her troubles. She didn't expect him to know about going viral. "In dense areas, far beyond the noise of traffic and chatter, I feel a peace. It quiets my anxieties. I'm not explaining it right.

"I don't fit in. Anyone, especially guys who went out of their way to be nice to me, were usually just using me to get to my famous parents. Oh, how I tried to bend my triangular edges. I hunched and bunched myself into a ball, trying my hardest to be a circle. At times, I made myself small, silent, unnoticeable. I got tired of the look people gave me when they find out I don't have a website. Or I don't display my happiness or sadness on the internet. I got treated like an alien. And I now know why I always *felt* different. You showed me that I am different. And I'm not alone in my uniqueness."

Selina stopped speaking. Instead, she used all of her focus to convey herself through their mental connection. She opened her memories. Bradly, her first boyfriend, used to snap secret photos of her and sell stories to the tabloids about her family. She allowed her feelings of awkwardness and non-acceptance to rise up her spine and into the link she shared with Augustus. Selina imparted similar memories.

Augustus maintained eye contact with her as he received her images. Respectfully, he did not attempt to hide the tears swaying on his eyelashes as she opened her feelings, fears, and hopes. The two stood motionless, their eyes locked on the other.

"Of course, a wolf would feel differently among dogs. Its instincts are exceptional. Its appearance and intelligence are far superior. The wolf will find no solace in their company. The dogs will never accept it, which is why wolves need to be with other wolves, if you can understand. You are Mother. You broke my chains. You are the founder of my freedom, and you've only had your powers for a few days." He smiled, shyly turning away from her face. "You will change this world. That is what my heart tells me. I…"

She kissed him. She crept closer to his lips until she could no longer control herself. There were other men in her past, but at this moment, she never felt closer to anyone in her entire life.

Augustus leaned into her, placing his hands on the small of her back. Greedily, he returned her affections but stopped abruptly. Wearing a dizzy expression, he touched his lips in disbelief.

"I choose you," she said quickly. "You are worthy of me. It is my verdict to reach, and I choose you."

He pulled her into his arms; he squeezed her tightly.

"I promise to be worthy of you, my queen," he whispered softly in her ear. "We are meant to be, but there is a promise I must fulfill."

Selina pulled away from him, confused.

"This feels like goodbye," she stated. "How can you say all those things and leave, knowing Edha is still out there?"

"You must learn who you are. *All* that you are. Only then can your choice be sound." Augustus spoke softly.

"Do you doubt my faith in you? Or is it that you don't have enough faith in yourself to stand *with* me?"

"That is a poor calculation of my affections," he argued. "I'd die for you."

"Then fight with me," she spoke vigorously. "We both saw that smile. I'm pretty sure the totems failed to compel Edha." A tense silence clouded the room. Augustus edgily avoided eye contact with Selina. His posture became stiff and awkward. Selina did not understand his change in behavior.

"I'm aware there's a need to meet my family; Laline's family," Selina said finally. "And I must learn my origin. I need to know more about my magic. Is it ancestral or elemental, like yours?" He raised his brows as if to speak, but she deliberately kept talking. "Also, I'm sure one of them can teach me how to focus my power, to defend myself and my family, which includes you." Her voice cracked. She looked away from him as fresh tears plopped down her cheeks. "You entered my life with such kindness and certainty, it swept me off my feet. You were the first to really see me, Laline. You protected me over and over; you fought for me. Recklessly chose me over yourself, over and over." Tears streamed from her eyes.

"Selina," he whispered in an apologetic tone. She fought the urge to tell him how she truly felt. In the few days together, he just about stole every bit of her heart. She studied his face for clues, hoping to decipher the reason he's leaving at the worst possible time. She feared facing Edha without him. More accurately, she quivered in horror at the thought of Augustus up against Edha alone. Yet the more Selina looked into his eyes, the more he avoided her stares. It hit her hard, like a sledgehammer. He meant to leave no matter what—whether she told him she loved him or not. Whether she *begged*, she cried, or asked him not to go. From what little she learned about mentally linking, she could tell his mind was made up. The rest he hid from her; a talent in which she practiced enough to recognize. And just like that, she pushed all of her feelings aside and chose to keep any further reservations to herself. He no longer needed to know.

"Come to think of it, you're right," Selina said unconvincingly as she wiped her tears away. "It's fine. I don't like it obviously, but hey, do what you gotta do."

"Thank you for understanding." He smiled. "I will find you again, I promise." He pressed his hands over hers. "We are meant to be together soon, my stars." With those words, he disappeared into the mirror world.

"Soon," Selina said to the empty seat where Augustus sat.

CHAPTER 28

THE REUNION

Soft, sprinkling snow landed gently in Augustus's hair. He playfully shook it off. It's been six weeks since he left Selina to embark on a secret journey. One he promised his dead sister he'd complete.

He looked up at the sky excitedly; convective clouds hovered above him. Even in partial moonlight, he still had a perfect view of the Mission Mountain peaks as part of the huge skyline. He stopped walking for a moment to relish in Montana's idyllic environment, an inviting change he cherished. He'd just began foraging the frosty hills of the National Bison Range, which is not allowed and can be downright dangerous for a person to do alone, at night, and after closing. However, Augustus needed the cover of darkness to achieve his task.

He took a deep breath. The air entered him crisp, pure, and clean, unlike the pollution he experienced in New York. He allowed himself to enjoy the open country for a few moments. Ironically, his thoughts brought him back to the assignment at hand. He decided it best to continue.

Dense clusters of rocky mountain juniper trees provided him with enough coverage to scatter about undetected. For both of their sakes: him and the one he intended to rescue, he needed to remain unseen.

One coyote yowled in the distance; two others joined it. And soon, the night became electric with sound and movement. The bitter-biting November cold ravaged on, freezing everything in its path except for Augustus. He possessed elemental magic, directly gifted to his ancestors by the spirits of the forest. Within his blood lies an enchantment, protecting him from extreme temperatures. If any creature can survive the night safely, it'd be him.

Knowing only that Jackson was taken somewhere in the northwest part of the United States, he decided to start his expedition in South Dakota. There, he navigated through miles of rolling prairies and badlands, a hard-rocky type of terrain of which he walked through with great difficulty. The raised geological deposits reminded him of miniature mountains, some knee-length, and others as tall as his chest. Climbing them took a great deal of effort after a while, but he knew he'd be alone out there in the dark. He couldn't risk anyone discovering him.

Dusk uncovered a jeweled sky filled with thousands of stars. He gazed upon them for hours wishing Selina were there with him. Yet he knew he couldn't risk her safety.

Next, he ventured through Wyoming's Black Hill Forest. Under a bright sapphire moon, he left no leaf unturned, looking for the bison Jackson may be trapped in. He walked through the deepest areas of the woodland, careful not to be detected by those who meant to harm him. He found himself both loving and hating the solitude of his journey. He supposed it'd been due to him both wanting to rescue Jackson and wanting to rush back to Selina.

A horned owl soared high across the Douglass fir trees. It spoke of a bison herd close by, he learned. Could he communicate directly to animals? No. But the forest does speak to those with skillful ears. The wind carries words. The brooks babble, and the trees rustle whispers to those who know their language. He understood its sound.

His heart leaped high in his throat. Could it be? Will he finally have his sister's dying wish fulfilled before daybreak?

A few yards up, he saw the herd asleep on the ground. He crept toward them carefully and quietly on his tip toes. His heartrate climbed, the closer he approached. His hands anxiously shook.

"*Jackson,*" he said telepathically over and over as he touched each of the bison. Much like the many herds before this one, the bison didn't seem alarmed by his contact. Most ignored him entirely. Since his power originated from spirits of the forest, nearly all animals trusted him. Perhaps his scent or gentle-natured aura established a mutual sense of safety.

He began to feel the familiar pang of disappointment when he reached the next to last one and did not sense a presence within.

"*Augustus?*" the final one answered as he touched the sleeping beast's forehead. The enormous oxlike animal stood up, totally erecting itself, indicating he heard the visitor's mental hails.

"*Jackson?*" Augustus cried telepathically, excitedly. He hugged the bison and was barely able to wrap his arms around the wooly creature. Augustus quickly brought Jackson's mind into his own, a practice only magical beings can accomplish.

The man inside the bison stood 6'6" in height. He had the brawn of a Viking warrior and the long blonde hair to match. Upon looking into his emerald-green eyes, Augustus could see how his sister fell madly in love with him. Overcome with joy, he hugged Jackson tightly.

"Christ, Brother, what happened to your eye?" Jackson asked of his late wife's, youngest sibling. Aside from the coagulated, nearly decaying-looking right eye, Jackson's last remaining relative seemed just as he remembered. Augustus's pale, thin features and his blue-black hair cascading past his shoulders instantly reminded him of his beloved Abigail.

"Good to see you too." Augustus laughed awkwardly, obviously embarrassed of his injury.

"How are you here?" Jackson asked seriously. "Are we free now? Has the curse ended for us?"

"Not quite." Augustus answered.

"Is this a visit then?"

"No. I've come to free you, Brother," Augustus confessed. "I've come to separate you from this animal, as I have been separated from mine."

"Okay," he said. "But I don't think you can do it all by yourself."

"I walk freely in my natural form. You do not see a cat before you, do you?" Augustus snarked.

"Yeah, but you might be a ghost haunting me," Jackson laughed again. "Or I might finally be losing it."

"Did you remember me missing an eye?"

"No. I suppose you're right. Apologies. I know what you're risking just by being here. Thank you." Augustus smiled at his brother-in-law's kind words. "May I ask, how did you get free?" Jackson queried.

"It's a long story. Come, the animal and I must enter the mirror world."

"Wait. Are we walking out of here?" he asked. Augustus answered with an uneasy nod. "I kinda wish you brought a truck," Jackson joked. "The animal is slow, too slow. And it tires easily."

"Then we shall travel at your pace and take many breaks," Augustus promised. At least we'll have more time to become better acquainted. It's been too long since I saw you last. I feared you dead." Augustus admitted.

"I feared the same." Jackson confessed. "More time. Okay, let's get to the meat of it. Start with how you got free." Jackson bellowed eagerly. Augustus laughed with his belly. He'd forgotten how humorous Jackson could be.

"Skip past beehive and straight to honey?" Augustus asked again. "Ok. I'll start at the beginning. One night while strolling the grounds, I felt the sunshine on my heart. And I knew... I knew my queen had come." Augustus said bashfully.

"Is this a story bout a girl?" Jackson interrupted.

"No. This story is about a warrior named Selina."

CHAPTER 29

THIS SHOULD BE INTERESTING

F at snowflakes fell like fluffy cotton balls, blanketing the earth in a soft white. Jackson, still trapped in the body of the bison, waited for Augustus to regain consciousness. The full moon above had long since reached its apex and did little to brighten the sky. In the black of night, he resisted sleep himself. Augustus mentioned earlier the two were nearing the edge of the Old Ten Scenic Byway in North Dakota. Currently, the trail of snowy hilltops remained quiet, desolate, and safe. Yet Jackson knew daylight brought out hikers, hunters, and anyone else with the possibility of potentially spotting them.

The last thing he needed was to get recaptured or worse, shot by the various hunters lurking in the woods for big game. He thought to nudge his brother-in-law but dare not risk further injury with the beast's lethal horns. He held the same reservations for his hooves to rouse the comatose man. Bison did not have the best eyesight, especially at night.

It had been seventeen days since Augustus *rescued* him from the bison range. Although admittedly, Jackson, in this moment, wished he hadn't come. The animals were safe there, far safer than traveling with someone oblivious to the dangers surrounding him. The two of them popped in and out of Augustus's mirror world, surfacing only for sustenance. If all went according to plan, he'd be free by now.

"We only need wait 'til Sunday," he remembered Augustus promising repeatedly. "It's when the *Long Night's Moon* begins." Jackson, at the time, didn't have the heart to express his doubts. He *wanted* to believe. Yet deep down, he knew December's cold moon, more commonly known as the Long night's moon, differed greatly from the lunar event that helped set him free.

Jackson knew Augustus needed to exhaust every possible option before he could deem his promise fulfilled, even in failure. And he hoped tonight's attempt at freeing him was the final one.

* * *

"It didn't work," Augustus said telepathically with a despondent expression after been unconscious for ninety minutes.

"No, it didn't," Jackson answered via their mental link. "The moon that freed you, the blood moon, is directly connected to the spirit world."

"Right," Augustus recalled, still seated in the snow. "Wait. You knew it wouldn't work, and you let me try anyway?"

"I wished by some miracle it worked, for your sake."

"For me? I don't understand."

"You gave it a good go, but it's time to take me back," Jackson said sternly.

"I can't."

"Brother, you must."

"But it's not safe there," Augustus protested.

"It's not safe out here with you," Jackson argued. "If any one of those hunters spotted me while you were out, I'm somebody's furry boots. I'm someone's lunch and dinner. I'm mounted over a fireplace next to a moose head. You can't protect me!" Augustus gasped at Jackson's harsh words.

"I promised Abigail I'd free you," he replied.

"She knows you did all you could. I do too! I'm forever grateful for your efforts. It's just too dangerous."

"If you were to allow me but one more chance?" Augustus begged on the bring of panic.

"What is there left to try? Honestly, haven't you attempted everything within your limits? It's over. Fold. Take me back already," Jackson demanded.

"That's precisely it." Augustus stood and waved them both into the mirror world. "I've exhausted all of my capabilities when it was not I who freed me."

"I think you might've hit your knocker on the way down." Jackson presumed.

"It makes perfect sense," Augustus said excitedly. "I delayed this inevitability, but I can no longer deny it."

"You're rambling."

"I need her. I need to bring her to us or us to her." Augustus declared.

"I hope you're not talking about Selina?"

"I am."

"The woman of whom you professed your love?"

"Yes." Augustus confirmed confused.

"And abandoned ten minutes later?"

"I didn't abandon her," he argued. 'I made a promise to save you."

"So why isn't she here with us?"

"This was my path, not hers." Augustus clarified.

"But that's not all, is it?" Jackson surmised.

"That is all that matters."

"If that were so, you wouldn't be shaking."

"You can't possibly tell with the eyes of that beast! You'd sooner walk into a tree. Again," Augustus joked.

"Then allow me to speak face-to-face, as I truly am," Jackson requested, and Augustus obliged. He brought his late sister's husband into his mind.

"Happy now?" Augustus asked, staring into the eyes of his towering brother.

"No," Jackson answered, completely fed up. "You need to take me back."

"It will be a success, you'll see." Augustus swore.

"What makes you think she'll help you? What makes you sure she'll even speak to you after what you did?"

"What I did? You mean find you? That's all I did."

"You told her you loved her. You basically swore your allegiance as a knight would a queen, and then you left like a coward." Jackson detailed.

"Should I not hold some allegiance to Abigail?"

"But that's not it." Jackson stood with his arms crossed over the other, like a parent would a fibbing child. "Admit it."

"I will not squabble over an assumption or presumption."

"Admit it!" he yelled, grabbing Augustus by his elbows and easily lifting him upward. "Both our lives hang in the balance here. Your story is lacking. Tell me the rest."

"FINE!" Augustus yelled back. "I left to find you for Abigail. And for me, also."

"Go on," Jackson nudged, dropping his brother to the ground.

"During the latest run-in with my captors, I sustained this injury. I am partially blind as a result." He remained on the ground; he did not want to see Jackson's face while describing his defeat. "I barely survived the encounter. Selina went against my wishes. I was prepared to perish but survived at her insistence."

"I understand the feeling," Jackson said, extending his hand to pull Augustus up. Augustus took it. "I remember a time I survived at your sister's insistence." Jackson pulled Augustus up from the ground. "You mean a lot to her too, so why isn't she here? Why did you part?"

"She opened her mind to me, and I saw... I felt her feelings for me."

"You speak as though it was a bad sight. A woman's love is sacred."

"During the battle, Edha told me I was the weakest of the nine. I fear it to be true, Brother. You accuse me of not protecting you, but it is HER I can't protect," Augustus said with great emphasis. "She is safer without me."

"I see," Jackson said. "What of the Aprīcōrum? Is this Edha one of their elders?"

"No, Edha cannot yield magic on her own. She uses dark objects. I don't know anything of the Aprīcōrum. I haven't felt their presence here."

"So, Selina defied the Aprīcōrum as well by freeing you."

"Unknowingly, of course, but it will not matter." Augustus said before sighing deeply.

"You still haven't explained why you left." Jackson pointed out.

"Love is self-forfeiting. My presence increases the chances of her jeopardizing her life for me. The thought makes me ill. She means everything to me."

"What makes you think Edha won't kill her anyway?"

"Edha wanted to siphon Selina's magic. Keep it for herself, in a glass orb. I do not believe the woman will kill Selina. She sees her as a victim, manipulated by me. If Edha succeeds, she will be a mightier opponent. She detests the nine with such a deep and black virility, none of us will be safe," Augustus confessed.

"Did you explain all this to Selina?"

"No. Weakness is unbecoming of a future mate," Augustus stated. Jackson laughed with his full belly. "Is my predicament comedic to you?"

"Love is about honesty and trust. I'm sure she thinks far worse of you now."

"I value your clarity of thought. What do you propose? Can I fix it?"

"I don't know. It's up to Selina. For now, I'd like to rest. Tomorrow we can begin searching for her."

"Do you mean it?" Augustus leaped joyfully. "You no longer want me to take you back?"

"No. I need to regain my freedom and join this fight. You need to focus on how to get your girl back, so she can help us." Augustus hugged Jackson tightly. He released Jackson from his mind so they both could get some much-needed rest

Jackson, as the bison, laid down first. Augustus stood staring out into the mirror world's oblivion.

This should be interesting, Jackson thought as he drifted off to sleep.

Enjoyed this book?

Visit www.tethysnightsky.com and sign up for our newsletter.

Follow us on
Twitter.com/TethysNightSky and
Facebook.com/TethysNightSky
for updates on the next installment:

Jackson's Redemption

Coming Soon in Fall 2021
Check out our other titles:

<u>The Fox Demon's Kiss</u> by Keri Moore available on Amazon, Apple, and Barnes and Noble for Nook.

ABOUT THE AUTHOR

LUNA STONE

Books were a constant in this author's home growing up. The local library was visited as much as the supermarket. Luna Stone was a child of the Berenstain Bears and Curious George. "Nothing enchants the spirit more than a great story," Stone says often. She supposed her love for writing began early too. Stone wrote her first story at age eight entitled, "Tall Like Me." The twelve-page book consisted of loose-leaf paper stapled together. In it amongst the crooked illustrations made with colored pencils existed a tale about a girl being bullied because of her height. Throughout Stone's school age years and well into college she enjoyed the works of Paulo Coelho, Stephen King, Angela Carter, James Bald- win, and hundreds more. The Curse of the Nine: Laline's Ascension is her first published novel. She is currently working on the sequel: Jackson's Redemption, at home in New York.

Want to know more?

Follow her on Twitter:
www.twitter.com/LunaStoneNYC